Denny Davis is retired and married with two grown-up children. He enjoys reading, mainly non-fiction, and helping his wife in the garden. He is interested in Military History, and History, generally. He lives in Wales.

This book is dedicated to my dear wife, who remained uncomplaining at my seemingly married to my word processor rather than her.

Denny Davis

A Visitation and Other Stories

Austin Macauley Publishers®
London • Cambridge • New York • Sharjah

A CIP catalogue record for this title is available from the British Library.

ISBN 9781035844753 (Paperback)
ISBN 9781035844760 (ePub e-book)

www.austinmacauley.com

First Published 2024
Austin Macauley Publishers Ltd®
1 Canada Square
Canary Wharf
London
E14 5AA

I acknowledge the debt I owe to the huge number of people I know and have known during my long life, who have unwittingly provided the inspiration for many of these stories.

Table of Contents

The Visitation

Ellen's small detached cottage, together with one other, lay at the end of a road which led from the village of Brockham and passed through a wood known as Tilley's Copse. The road was more of a lane really, although it was tarmacked.

After 22 years in the army as a military policewoman sergeant followed by 18 years running a team of security personnel for a private company, Ellen was eagerly looking forward to some peace and quiet, tending the garden which was already well stocked with roses and other flowers.

She had been a bit dubious at first as to whether or not she should buy the cottage. The price seemed over-reasonable and the previous owners, the Robinsons, seemed over-eager to sell. A full structural survey soon put Ellen's mind at rest and she soon moved in, very pleased at her good luck. She had never married even though she had never been short of admirers or dance partners in the mess. Independence was Ellen's forte.

The day after moving in, she decided to acquaint herself with her neighbour. A knock on the front door soon produced another lady, a few years older than Ellen, who invited her in out of the cold January day, and introduced herself as Jane.

Over cups of tea and biscuits, Jane said she was a widow with one married daughter who had emigrated years before to Australia with her husband and had their children there. Like Ellen, Jane was pretty independent but kept in touch with her family by telephone and letter.

By and by Ellen raised the subject of her 'bargain' cottage and the eagerness of the Robinsons to sell. Jane, biting her lower lip, went quiet for a moment then said: "That was because of the ghost."

"Ghost?" queried Ellen, choking on a biscuit, "What ghost?"

"I don't know," replied Jane. "They said they saw a ghost but I never saw one and nobody else did either. People hereabouts thought they were odd and tended to avoid them. It started last year, about the beginning of August. I think they'd been here about five years before that."

"Well, I'm not scared of any old ghost," retorted Ellen. "I bet I saw worse than that when I was in the army." With that, she thanked Jane for the tea and chat, invited her round to her cottage and took her leave.

One afternoon a few days later, Ellen was washing some woollens in the kitchen sink when she saw a figure entering her back gate. It was a man dressed as an airman with black fur-lined boots, a blue uniform and a yellow Mae West around his neck. *Oh dear,* she thought, *I do hope there hasn't been an accident.*

From the time it took her to dry her hands he should have been at her door, but there was no knock. She opened the door to find herself looking at the closed back gate – no sign of any airman. She went out and walked around the cottage. Nothing. *I must be seeing things,* she thought, *all this talk of ghosts with Jane.* She made a note of it in her diary though.

The succeeding days passed uneventfully enough, and a few weeks later on a nice March spring afternoon, Ellen was busily working in her back garden, generally tidying things up and noting the daffodils and bluebells which grew in profusion with the roses. Suddenly, she felt the hairs on the back of her neck stiffen and a sort of temporary immobility come into her limbs. She straightened up and whirled round only to be confronted by the same man still dressed as before, an airman. He was very handsome with blue eyes and sandy-coloured crinkly hair.

"Who are you and what do you want?" she asked firmly. The man didn't reply but just smiled, at the same time holding out his right hand. Instinctively, she reached out to take it but found herself grasping at thin air. "Well?" she said in her best sergeant's voice, "what is it?"

There was no answer; he continued to smile with his open hand out. A few seconds more and he faded away, leaving Ellen looking at the fence which separated her garden from Jane's.

Feeling rather put out but not frightened, Ellen went indoors for a bracing cup of tea with a splash of whisky in it, her brows knitted in thought. *A ghost?* Such a thing had never happened to her before. Then something struck her, causing her to go for her diary. *Yes!* The last time she had seen the airman was on February 4th and today was March 4th. So the same day each month! She rushed round to tell Jane; the two women had become good friends by now.

On hearing what Ellen had to say, Jane took a step backwards and clutched at her throat, a wary look in her eyes. Ellen noticed and said: "I don't mean to scare you and I've never seen a ghost before. I'm certainly not scared and I obviously wasn't dreaming the first time I saw him."

"You've seen him before?" queried Jane.

"Yes," replied Ellen, "on the 4th of last month. If he keeps this up then he's due to reappear on the 4th of next month. Will you please be with me to see if you can see him too? He can't hurt us."

Jane hesitated and thought whether if she get involved. But Ellen looked so strong and self-willed and certainly not scared.

"Alright," she said reluctantly at last. "I'll give it a go."

The days dragged by with Jane beset with self-doubts. At last, she said to herself: "A promise is a promise so I'm not going to chicken out." No such qualms were part of Ellen's makeup. In fact, she was rather looking forward to the next encounter – assuming it happened.

April 4th arrived and the afternoon found both women waiting at Ellen's open back door. The airman duly appeared and walked silently towards them. "He's here," said Ellen in a whisper, "handsome, isn't he?"

"I can't see anything," said Jane, causing Ellen to frown at her.

The airman came up to the door then, as before, broke out into his silent smile whilst holding out his open right hand. Again Ellen asked: "What do you want?" But there was no answer and he faded away leaving her looking at her back gate.

"There!" she exclaimed, "Did you see?"

"No, I didn't," replied Jane, "but I must admit I felt something, a kind of heaviness in the air."

Ellen shut the door and put the kettle on while Jane sat lost in thought. When tea and cake were on the table she said: "You say he held his hand out each time, is that right?"

"Yes," said Ellen, "his right hand."

"That's it!" said Jane excitedly. "You've got something he wants which is why only you can see him and it must be the reason why only the Robinsons could see him. There's something in this house he wants!"

"But what could that be?" replied Ellen with a puzzled look on her face. "The house was completely empty when I moved in and I hoovered everywhere before moving my stuff in."

Jane went silent again, then: "What about outside? The shed for instance?"

"Not much in there," said Ellen doubtfully, "apart from an old chest of drawers and my gardening tools."

"Well, let's look anyway," said Jane who was really into the spirit of things by now. So tea and cake both consumed the two ladies adjourned to Ellen's shed.

It was a small wooden shed just six feet by four and, as Ellen had said, contained just a few tools and an old, small chest of drawers pushed up against a wall. An examination of the latter produced a hammer with a broken handle and a very rusty tenon saw but nothing else.

Then Ellen noticed something. The chest of drawers was not quite against the wall, there was a gap behind it. She pulled it away and both women heard something fall down. Ellen got her rake and hooked it out. A flying helmet complete with integral headphones and trailing leads! Its leather was stiff and dusty and the sight of it caused both women to gasp.

"That's it!" exclaimed Jane, "that's what he wants!"

"You could well be right," said Ellen, "but how do you give anything to a ghost? And how did it get here?"

Back in the house, Ellen used a damp cloth to wipe the dust from the helmet whilst thinking hard, then said: "This year is 1991 so last year was the fiftieth anniversary of the Battle of Britain and you said it was about August when the Robinsons said they first saw him."

"Yes," said Jane, "the beginning of August, I think."

With heads together, they both examined the helmet for some clue as to its owner. It was there, faintly written in ink inside, the word 'Warren'.

"So now we have his name," said Ellen with satisfaction. "Now what?"

"There's a half-decent library in Branford," replied Jane after some thought. "We could try there."

"Good idea, we'll go in the morning," said Ellen determinedly. "Another cup of tea?"

There was no library in the village and Branford was the nearest town of any size. The two ladies remained lost in thought as Ellen's little car took them there. The library had its own car park and they were soon glad to get into the warmth of the large room which was the reference section. A question to the librarian led them to a large book titled *The Battle of Britain in Detail.* They took it to a nearby table.

Ellen consulted the index. There were three Warrens listed but only one of them had the *d* for 'deceased' next to his name. Page 73 and Ellen quickly turned to it. "There he is!" she said, pointing to a photograph of a smiling young man holding a flying helmet.

Jane stared. “Wow,” she said at last, “he is handsome isn’t he? Or rather was. I bet that helmet he’s holding is the one you have!”

The top of the page bore the date 4th August 1940. Ellen then pointed to the caption. It read: “Hurricane P69448 shot down by return fire from a German bomber at 15:10 hours. Crashed in Tilley’s Copse near Brockham, Surrey. Pilot Officer Donald Warren, despite severe injuries, managed to seek help at a nearby cottage, but tragically succumbed to his injuries in the local hospital two days later. He is buried in the local cemetery.”

“It must have been your cottage he got to,” said Jane, “and left his helmet behind. Now he’s come back for it.”

Ellen flicked through other pages. Maps, plans, photographs of crashed aircraft and many more smiling young men. “What a waste,” she muttered, “what a stupid bloody waste.” The two ladies then left the library, both pondering on those momentous events of so long ago. While they had been children at the time, they both had many memories of the fear, noise, destruction and privations.

Back in the car, Ellen sat lost in thought for a few minutes. Then her face brightened and she said: “I know what we’ll do. We’ll find his grave and bury the helmet in it. What do you think, are you game?”

“Yes,” replied Jane, who was beginning to enjoy the adventure. It was such a change from her normal routine. “But,” she went on, “you’ll never get permission and even if you did it would get publicised and one of those collectors would dig it up and steal it.”

Ellen looked her in the eye. “I wasn’t going to ask permission.” She said determinedly.

Jane raised her eyebrows. “Oh,” she said in surprise, but quickly entering into the spirit of things went on, “Well let’s go and find the grave then. Just pretend we’re just looking around; don’t want to be too obvious.”

Ellen started the car and Jane directed her to the cemetery. It was larger than Ellen had expected as three local villages had been using it for centuries. Dotted about here and there amongst the memorials was the odd Commonwealth War Graves Commission headstone. Jane found the one they were looking for. Pilot Officer Warren’s details were there, etched into the stone and surmounted by the Royal Air Force Eagle. The two friends noted its position then went on their way.

Back in Ellen’s cottage, the plan was hatched. “We obviously need to go at night,” observed Ellen, “and there’ll need to be a moon as we daren’t show lights.” Her diary showed a full moon in a weeks’ time.

"Let's hope it's not cloudy," remarked Jane.

They were in luck and well wrapped up against the chilly night the two ladies on a mission set off, in Jane's car this time. In the boot were Ellen's small spade, a plastic bag and a bottle of water. Ellen nursed the helmet in her lap, safely sealed in a plastic bag with copious amounts of sticky tape to protect it from damp and insects.

They reached the cemetery, all quiet and the memorials shining white in the moonlight. They quickly found the grave and Ellen carefully removed a square of turf with her spade then dug down as deep as she was able, piling the spoil on to the plastic bag. The helmet was reverently placed in the hole, the spoil tipped back in, trodden down and some of the water sprinkled onto it. More water was splashed over the underside if the turf which was then carefully replaced and the remaining water sprinkled over it. There was no sign of anybody having been there.

"We ought to say something," whispered Jane.

"The Lord's Prayer will have to do," whispered Ellen in return.

Two heads were bowed and the words whispered. Then Ellen said: "Look after him God." After all those years in the army, she couldn't get out of the habit of issuing orders. Their mission completed, the two friends then left with a final backwards glance at the last resting place of a young man who had given his all.

Ellen never saw the ghost again but that wasn't quite the end of the story. She went back to the library and used their photocopier to make an enlargement of Pilot Officer Warren's photograph. She had this framed and hung it in her little sitting room, a permanent reminder of the time she helped a hero to find peace.

Where There's a Will

Mr Jennings of Jennings, Worsely and Jennings, attorneys at law, removed his spectacles and looked up from the paper on his desk at the expectant faces of the eight people seated before him. The faces belonged to the four children of Julius Kingmann, deceased, and their spouses. Eldest was John who was married to Mary, next came Helga with her husband Ken, then Greta and Walter. Finally there was Luke and his wife Doreen.

Julius had fled from Germany with his parents before the war. Although the cruelty against the Jews had not reached the small town where they lived, his parents had heard enough about it for them to get out while they could. They'd had no trouble selling their thriving general store and soon started another in London where they'd settled.

In due course, Julius married and inherited the business which he soon changed into a discount store, items just left in their cardboard cartons with the prices marked in crayon or felt tip on their outsides for customers to help themselves. This kept overheads and prices low, and under the name 'Discount King' the business boomed, so much so that at the time of his death Julius had branches scattered throughout the country. None of his children had chosen to work in the business and he'd been a widower for some fifteen years.

Mr Jennings cleared his throat and spoke: "As you know, Julius was a personal friend of mine and entrusted me to draw up his last will and testament according to his wishes. His will is quite straightforward but there is a twist in it which I'll come to in a minute. Julius' early life wasn't easy so he has left a task for you to perform, or should I say overcome, if you are to inherit his very considerable estate, including all his stores, without undue expense. Firstly, his housekeeper/gardener, the Simpsons, are to have fifty thousand pounds free of all taxes and duties. The rest of the estate to be divided into four equal parts and each part set up in the manner of a trust fund, one for each of you, the income of which will be considerable and will save a huge amount of death duties which the estate, if left as one unit, would accrue."

"That sounds straightforward enough," said Helga, who was an accountant, "so what's the snag?"

"I was coming to that," said Mr Jennings sternly, who didn't like to be interrupted. He held up the paper. "This is a copy of the will. Probate will not accept a copy so you need to find the original which Julius insisted on retaining himself, a most unusual procedure, if I may say so. If the original is not found, then Julius will be regarded as having died intestate and the whole estate will be lumped together as it were, incurring very heavy death duties. This will necessitate the sale of all, or nearly all, his stores. There will be some residue, of course, but this will be far less profitable to you all, especially as you will doubtless feel honour bound to pay the Simpsons their fifty thousand pounds. You have six months to find the original will as that is the maximum time the treasury will allow."

Mr Jennings then sat down while the eight people present looked at each other. Helga spoke again: "All we have to do is find the will. Shouldn't be too hard."

At this, Mr Jennings produced a white envelope from a drawer and gave it to Helga, saying: "Julius gave me this with the will copy."

Helga tore it open. Inside the envelope was a single sheet of white paper on which was printed just two words 'The Desk'. Helga repeated the words and held the paper up. "He must mean his old desk," she said, "It must be in there."

Thanking Mr Jennings, they all left and made their way to Julius' house. Mrs Simpson opened the door even though Luke and Doreen had keys because they lived there, she providing companionship for Julius in his last years while he worked as an insurance underwriter. Luke had married late and Doreen was rather younger than him. They had one child, Mark, aged ten who was a keen stamp collector. His collection was that of a typical child's, very few complete sets as his pocket money didn't stretch to the high values and the local sweet shop held its own attractions. The stamp he most coveted was a penny black but possession of one seemed a long way in the future. Now, in a corner of his grandfather's study, he sat at a small table with stamps, albums, tweezers, hinges and magnifying glass all spread before him. He looked up as the eight adults entered the room and descended on the old roll-top desk that stood in one corner.

The desk wasn't locked even though the key was in it. Greta opened it to reveal a great many papers stuffed into the pigeon holes and the three drawers. The two cupboards revealed more.

"I suggest we split this lot into four," she said, "and take a pile each." So it was done, and envelopes with stamps on being given to a grateful Mark after they and their contents had been carefully examined for clues.

The search produced nothing and the room went silent with eight people sitting on the floor, surrounded by bills and all sorts of other papers. Then Mary had a brainwave. She pulled the middle drawer out and, sure enough, there was another white envelope taped to the outside back of it. "Aha!" she cried triumphantly, "what's this?"

"The will, I hope," said Ken.

But it wasn't. Just another sheet of white paper with just three words printed on it. Mary read them out. "Oh dear! Gasometer," she read.

"Oh no," exclaimed John with a sigh. "Don't tell me he's hidden it near a gasometer. They are, or were, all over the place and most of them are gone now."

"Julius would have known that," said Walter.

"What's a gasometer?" piped up Mark.

John said: "Before we had natural gas we used to make our own."

"Here we go," muttered Doreen. Seven pairs of eyes turned heavenwards as John continued: "It was made from coal and there was a large gas works in our town; it was on both sides of the road. There was a railway line going into it and an overhead monorail. The coal was brought in by a train of coal trucks pulled by a small steam engine. It dumped some of it on one side of the road for coal merchants to buy then went across the road, holding all the traffic up, and dumped the rest there. Then the coal was loaded into ovens and baked which caused it to release gas. The gas was filtered then stored in gasometers which were also called gas holders. These were like huge drums and were usually in two parts like a telescope. The top part could slide up and down and was suspended in water to stop the gas getting out. It was very heavy and this provided the pressure of the gas which could be controlled by valves. The residue left in the ovens was called coke and after being cooled with water was taken back across the road by the monorail and dumped with the coal, also for coal merchants to buy."

He stopped and Doreen muttered: "Old windbag."

The eight adults then turned to the matter in hand. They went to the wall where a large map of Britain was pinned. Coloured pins were stuck in various towns. These indicated the location of Julius' stores and their colours indicated their profitability. There were sixteen of them.

"That's four each," said Walter. "I suggest we spend our weekends and spare time searching each town to see whether any of them have gasometers still standing and if not consulting local histories in their libraries for the locations of any that have now been demolished." As no one could think of anything better this was agreed upon with more than a few groans.

"We'll need to keep in contact with each other," said Greta, "so don't forget your mobiles and chargers."

"We'll need to meet back here," observed Ken. He consulted his diary. "I suggest Saturday, the 14th of October, as the deadline. It is a month after that and we'll have time to think of something else if this doesn't work."

The four couples then went their separate ways and their quest began, Luke and Doreen leaving Mark with the Simpsons each weekend.

The 14th of October found the four tired and dispirited couples back at the house, all considerably out of pocket what with travelling, overnight accommodation and restaurant meals.

"Well, that's that," said Mary, "now what?"

Nobody had an answer and the atmosphere became one of silent gloom. She picked up the paper with "Oh dear! Gasometer," written on it, now quite well-thumbed as each of the eight had examined it at one time or another. She threw it down on the table where mark sat with his stamp albums. Idly he picked it up and looked at it through his magnifying glass.

"It's wrong," he said at last.

"What's wrong?" asked his father.

"It's the zero, Dad," replied Mark, "it's different."

Luke picked up the paper and the magnifying glass and used it to look closely at the paper, the others staring at him expectantly as he knitted his brows in concentration. Suddenly his face cleared. "I've got it!" he cried in triumph. "The zero of gasometer has been written in a purple ink while the rest of it is black. You can only see it through a magnifying glass! If you remove the zero it says 'gas meter'! That's what the 'Oh dear!' meant, to draw our attention to the O!"

A stunned silence ensued followed by a stampede for the door. The resultant log jam being untangled, they rushed on.

"Where's the gas meter?" someone shouted.

"Outside," said Luke, "get the key, Doreen."

From a drawer in the kitchen, Doreen produced a flat oblong of plastic with a cylinder at one end with triangular cut-outs at each end. Outside, they found a small door set into the wall into which the key fitted. Opening it revealed a gas meter in a recess. There was just enough room behind it for Doreen's slim fingers and she drew out a third white envelope which bore in beautiful copperplate writing the inscription: "Last Will and Testament of Julius Kingmann."

The recess door was re-locked and the group returned to the study in trembling anticipation. Doreen carefully withdrew a paper from the envelope. Opening it she cried: "This is it! The will!"

Luke turned to his son. "Well done, Mark," he said excitedly, "this means we're rich!"

"Oh," replied Mark, somewhat bewildered by all the fuss. "Do you think I could have a penny black?"

"You certainly can," said his smiling father, "and a two penny blue as well!"

Two Gnomes

Hello! My name is Jock which should tell you where I come from. I also have another name which is Cairn terrier which should tell you what I am. I do not like the 'Terrier' bit because it sounds like 'Terror' and I'm not scared of anything. I even bark at the big dog next door when he passes our front gate. He just looks at me and grins.

I live in a nice, warm house with four people. My master takes me for long walks and I got to know all the people in the street that way. His wife, my mistress, feeds me with something she calls 'Kennomeat'. I know it's written on the tin but I can't read, can I? Their two children play with me in the large back garden sometimes and their friends join in too. Everybody seems to like me which is nice.

I can get into the small front garden through a flap in the front door, so I can come and go there when I please.

There are two things I hate. One is bath night. I really don't know why I have to be half drowned at regular intervals and made to feel really miserable and I can't get out of it as the family have found all my hiding places. I must admit though that I do feel better when I'm dry again. The other much hated thing is: The Gnome!

The gnome sits in the middle of our lawn in the back garden with that fixed, very annoying, grin on his face. I often give him a good barking to but he won't get up and run away so I can chase him and nip his ankles. He just sits there in his silly green trousers, red jacket, yellow shirt and blue cap. I look for him every time I can in the hope that he might have gone but no, he's always there mocking me. Grrrrrr!

One day, I heard the family talking about something called a 'circus'. They seemed quite excited about it, especially the children, and said they would all go to see it, whatever it was. They didn't mention taking me.

The day, or rather evening, arrived and off they all went, leaving me with the hallway and front garden to explore. I went outside. It was a chilly, clear night but the lamppost outside our house gave plenty of light. I did my usual rounds. No cat smell (I forgot that was my third pet hate) and found the gate hadn't been properly latched. A push with my nose and I was out. Freedom!

First port of call was the lamppost. A quick sniff told me another dog had been there. What a cheek! It was my lamppost! I quickly cocked a back leg and did what was required to blot him out. Plenty of other places to sniff at but then I noticed another gnome! This one was much bigger than the one in our garden and he was moving! He was dressed in a similar rubbish way and had a silly grin painted on his face. He was getting out of a downstairs window of a house up the road, which I thought was odd. But now was my chance!

Emitting my best growl, I scampered up the road, went into the gate and got him as he was coming down the path. I went for his ankles but caught a trouser leg. He tried to bat me away, saying: "Gerroff ya mutt! Sling yer 'ook!" and other things I won't repeat. I let go and gave him a good barking, dashing at his ankles every time he tried to get past me.

All this noise brought the neighbours out (they hadn't all gone to the circus). There were several of them. No, I can't count but I once saw a dog on the TV who could. I thought he was stupid. (Dog's golden rule: never let them see how clever you can be or else you'll have to work for your Kennomeat). One said: "What are you doing here? You must be a clown from the circus." (I can only guess that 'clown' is what they call big gnomes).

"I ain't doin' nothing," he said, "I just come out for some air."

"Then what are you doing in the Brown's garden?" asked the neighbour as he held on to my collar.

"Nothin' 'onest, mister," he replied.

"I don't believe you," said the neighbour. "Call the police, Jim," he said to one of the others. "And you stay where you are," he ordered the big gnome they called a clown.

Jim pulled one of those little box things from his pocket, poked it a few times and talked to it. A few minutes later, a car pulled up and two men dressed in black got out. Policemen, I supposed. Their car had big writing on the side but, as I said earlier, I can't read.

After a bit more talk one of the policemen searched the big gnome they called a clown and produced a long flat box from his pocket. The neighbours crowded round when he opened it and lifted out an ornate spoon. "What's this then?" He said in a stern voice.

A lady said: "I know what it is. It's an antique christening spoon which was given to the Brown's daughter when she was born. Solid silver, that is."

"Right," said the policeman, "down to the station with you." As the big gnome they called a clown moved forward, I lunged at him but the hold on my collar was too good. "Bleedin' vicious 'e is," he said, "wants puttin' down." I don't know what that meant but it didn't sound nice.

"Oh no," replied the neighbour, patting my head. "He's a hero, aren't you Jock?" The two policemen and the big gnome they called a clown got into the police car and went. The neighbour took me home, put me in the garden and made sure the gate was latched. Fun over, I wished it could have gone on longer.

The next day, a policeman came and told my family all about it while I listened from the comfort of my basket. Apparently, the big gnome they called a clown did his act early which gave him a good three hours to change his shoes for trainers then on dark winter's nights scout round the neighbourhood to see if there were any houses he could burgle while their occupants were at the circus – unless they had a dog, of course. They found quite a hoard in his caravan.

The policeman went and everybody made a fuss of me which was very nice. I didn't get Kennomeat that night but instead got a large, juicy and very tasty chunk of some other meat.

I needed a snooze after that so I lay in front of the fire with my head on my paws and thought about that other gnome in our garden. *So they can move,* I thought to myself, *I need to try harder. I'll give him a really good barking to tomorrow, then we'll see.* And with that happy thought I drifted off to sleep.

Just a Little Old Lady?

Maud felt quite put out when the Mini shot into the parking space she was just passing and intended to reverse into. "Oh hell," she muttered to herself. After driving round the block three times in her little Clio looking for a space, she'd now lost the one she'd found.

Maud didn't usually get angry at anything, being a very reserved, placid type of person. The feeling of resentment that arose in her now, together with not a little pique, was a rare exception. She determined to say something!

"Excuse me," she said to the young man who jumped out of the Mini. "You've stolen my place, I was here first."

Surprised, he stared at her for a few seconds, then a grin spread slowly over his face. "Tough," he replied. "First come first served, I'm afraid."

"Well, I think you should move," retorted Maud. "You could have parked in the main car park and walked. You look fit enough."

The grin spread into a smile: "Sorry, old love, I'm staying right here."

Maud didn't know whether it was the condescension in his voice or the 'old love' that did it. All she knew was that she suddenly felt a strong emotion rising within her, like a large air bubble rising from the hidden depths of a stagnant pond. Anger! In a sudden impulse she swung her handbag at the smirking face before her, neatly planting it on the left side of his head and sending him sprawling over the Mini's bonnet.

Horror! "What have I done?" said Maud to herself as she dropped her handbag and put her hands to her mouth. The young man was howling! But wait! The howling was of laughter, not distress, as the young man leant on his elbows on the bonnet of the Mini and, with head in hands, laughed until the tears ran.

Suddenly, a voice – a loud voice: "oi!" it shouted, "how dare you belt my son!" The voice came from the back seat of the Mini and it emanated from a lady who was every bit as old as Maud.

“I’ll belt you,” said the old lady in the Mini as she struggled to get out. But her struggle appeared to be fruitless as the Mini was a two-door one.

Maud quickly sized up the situation. Her Clio was blocking her side of the road and other cars which had been forced to swerve round it tooted at her angrily. Discretion being the better part of valour, Maud picked up her handbag, rammed her hat further on to her head, jumped into her Clio and drove off.

To her surprise she felt elated. *Didn’t know I had it in me,* she thought and went on, *I’ll do the shopping tomorrow and just let that damned butcher try to sell me fatty meat again!*

The worm had turned!

A Taste of Fruit?

We must all eat five per day. So say nutritional and other experts. Some say seven but I think five is enough for anybody. By five, they don't mean five chocolate eclairs, T-bone steaks or whatever else takes your fancy, they mean five pieces of fruit and vegetables.

This didn't bother Gerald; he loved fruit and vegetables, especially apricots.

Every Saturday he'd go to the market with his parents and select seven apricots, one for each day of the week. Those that were not quite ripe would be by the time the end of the week was reached.

One Saturday it rained. Not just what one might call normal rain but a real downpour. Things were quickly bundled into shopping bags, then a speedy dash to the car.

At home the things were unpacked and, to his horror, Gerald found one of his ripe apricots had been squashed into a pulp, soaking the bottom of its paper bag. What to do, waste it? Then Gerald had a brainwave. Why not try to grow his own? The rain had stopped so, with his father's permission, Gerald dug a hole in a corner of the garden and buried the apricot.

Each day he checked the area and one day he was rewarded with the appearance of a thin, little white shoot with just a trace of green at it its upper part. Gerald called his dad. "It's growing!" he said excitedly.

"Yes," said his dad, "but it looks weak. It needs feeding, there's some in the shed."

"No thanks, Dad," replied Gerald, "I want to do this myself."

Gerald hadn't spent any of his pocket money yet, he had been too wrapped up with his apricot plant. So now he nipped to the local shop on his bicycle and bought a large jar of squeeze-bottle Marmite.

Back home, he carefully unearthed the little shoot, its pulp now a grey mass, and squirted the Marmite into the hole. Then he removed the top of the bottle and rinsed out the residue, finally replacing the shoot and carefully re-filling the hole.

It worked! The little plant thrived and grew sturdy and quite tall. Winter was approaching and Gerald's father warned him against frost and how it could kill young plants. Gerald thought about that then came up with a solution.

In the shed was an old sheepskin jacket which his father didn't wear any more. Gerald lifted it down, surprised at how heavy it was. *That'll break the plant,* he thought, then came up with another solution.

Leaving the jacket where it was, he rushed up to his room, got his Meccano set out and made a rectangular frame. Back in the garden, he placed that over the little plant then covered it with the jacket. He did this each evening when a frost was forecast, removing the jacket each morning before going to school or waiting until lunch-time if the frost was exceptionally severe. The plant continued to thrive. So much so that Gerald had to extend his Meccano frame twice. Throughout the next spring and summer it grew into a miniature tree, some three feet high. By the next winter, it was big enough to withstand anything nature could throw at it so Gerald was able to dispense with the sheepskin jacket and his Meccano frame.

By the second autumn, the great day had arrived. Apricots had appeared and one or two were ready to eat! In the presence of his admiring parents, and with great anticipation, Gerald carefully picked one and took a large bite. He immediately grimaced, spat it out and dropped the apricot.

So believe me, dear reader, when I tell you that Marmite flavoured apricots do not taste nice!

Not a Good Start

Eva and Jack were very much looking forward to their forthcoming marriage. They'd been engaged for 18 months which they both thought was long enough for anybody, but it had given them enough time to save for a deposit on a somewhat rundown terraced house and obtain a joint mortgage.

Jack and his brother had utilised all their spare time working on the house and now it was – apart from the garden – ready for Eva and Jack to move into on their wedding day, much to the relief of both sets of parents!

As to the wedding itself, Jack, with the help of his brother, insisted on making all the arrangements apart from the guest invitations which he left to Eva. The local village hall was booked, likewise the caterer and Eva's younger brother jumped at the chance of providing the disco. Jack ordered a new suit and Eva and her mother chose the wedding dress.

The honeymoon would be for just one week at a very nice hotel which was some distance away. Jack had spent some time looking for such a hotel which obviously had to be one they could afford, of reasonable quality and, most importantly, have a sea frontage. A recommendation from a work colleague followed by a visit settled the matter.

The siting of the hotel was important because of Jack's boat. Being a keen fisherman, he liked nothing better than to chug out to sea with a couple of mates together with fishing gear, lager in a cool box and Ginster's pasties. To any outside onlooker it could easily appear that the lager was more important than the fishing!

The arrangements were simply thus: the wedding would take place on a Saturday morning. The night before, Jack would take his and Eva's normal clothes to the hotel room ready for them to change into when they arrived the next day. After the reception, Jack and Eva would ride the five miles to the harbour in a taxi then motor along the coast in the boat to the hotel, no doubt accompanied by the shouts and good luck wishes of other boat owners.

The great day dawned hot, windless and not a cloud in the sky. The wedding, food and disco all went very well, then Jack and Eva departed to a host of waves, good wishes and a few tears.

The taxi dropped them off at the harbour, turned round and departed leaving Jack and Eva to cross the road, she holding up the hem of her dress.

They reached the quayside where they were confronted by a plethora of small boats sitting on a sea of mud. "You idiot!" exclaimed Eva, "the tide's out!"

"Oh God!" cried Jack, "the one thing I forgot to check!"

There was no one else about. The buildings behind them were warehouses, closed for the weekend. Nothing for it but to walk back to the town, nearly a mile away. "In these shoes?" wailed Eva. "Well, I don't want to wait here on my own so I'll have to take them off, thanks to you!"

They set off, Eva holding up her dress and carrying her shoes yelling "Ouch!" every time she trod on a stone.

Finally, Jack picked her up and early evening shoppers were treated to the unusual sight of a perspiring groom carrying his bride. A taxi was sought and turned out to be the same one which had dropped them. The driver thought the situation so funny that he conveyed them to the hotel without charge. Eva didn't share the joke, remaining grim-faced throughout the journey.

In their hotel room at last, the pair changed in silence then looked at one another. As one they burst out laughing and continued to do so for at least five minutes before falling onto the bed in each other's arms.

The honeymoon, together with the marriage, was a great success so there we leave Jack and Eva with a good story to tell their children!

Saved!

Fred stood, as he always did, during his after-breakfast walk and looked lovingly at the few small fields that now constituted his domain. Everything had worked out fine even though there was a pang of regret caused by neither of his sons wanting to become farmers like himself.

At 55 years of age, Fred had sold most of his land to the farmer next door, using the money to put his sons through college and university. The renting out of the farm buildings to local traders provided a nice income for himself and his wife, Pat. He still kept a few livestock to 'keep his hand in' as it were and these were more like pets than anything else.

He arrived home to be greeted by his wife waving a letter. "Looks official," she said pointing to the 'OHMS' printed on it.

"Busybodies," said Fred, "what do they want now?" He opened and read it, went white and dropped into a chair.

"What is it?" asked a concerned Pat.

"They want to dig up our farm," he replied, handing her the letter. In essence, it said oil was suspected to lie beneath and, if true, the farm may well be liable for compulsory purchase.

"Oh my dear," exclaimed Pat, "where will we go?"

"I'm not taking this lying down," said Fred as he quickly regained his composure. "You note it also says plans will be displayed at the town hall for people to comment on. I'll comment all right."

Fred then set about enlisting local support which culminated in a public meeting in the same town hall three weeks after the plans had been displayed and commented on. The council chairman presided. Fred had plenty of support but there was opposition too. Local shopkeepers and publicans saw opportunities for increased business, not to mention builders who looked at Fred's fields with hungry eyes. The council was against Fred too, plenty of job opportunities not to mention council taxes from houses and other buildings.

But against Fred's and Pat's hopes, the axe fell and a second OHMS letter announced exploratory drilling would begin in six weeks' time.

The week before a very sad Fred had stood and looked again at his land which had been his home all his life. The few livestock happily grazing, the magnificent oak tree and the dead one next to it which he'd never had the heart to cut down. The hum of activity from the buildings. He imagined it all gone and shuddered.

He sadly walked towards the house, but as he approached it Pat came running out shouting: "Fred! We're saved!" They met and she pulled a third OHMS letter out of her apron pocket. Fred took it and read that there had been a change of plan and the farm would thus be left in peace.

"What change of plan?" queried a mightily relieved Fred.

The answer came the next day. It was all over the media. The decision of Honda to vacate their Swindon plant in 2021 had caused the government to step in to compulsory purchase it.

The next two years would be spent in designing an all-British electric car which would be built in the factory. The same two years would be spent improving our infrastructure which will not currently support a large number of electric cars. This would not only provide employment but would greatly reduce the air pollution problem and give us an all-British car industry again. Demand for oil greatly reduced!

"Well," said Fred raising his glass, "isn't technology wonderful!"

The Future?

"Forbidden Planet," is a science fiction film made in 1956. Despite its age, the story and special effects still stand up well.

It is set in the future where we have colonised planets outside our own solar system. A problem has arisen on one of them and a spaceship is sent to investigate.

When they arrive, they find only two people left alive, the others having died by something unknown. The two that are left are professor Morbius and his daughter, Altaira. Morbius has discovered that the whole planet has been turned into a vast machine by a long-vanished race called Krell, leaving a vast archive of their knowledge.

Using this archive, plus his own considerable intellect, Morbius has constructed a lovely garden full of animals which are all very tame, even a tiger, then continued examining the archive and carrying out certain experiments.

He decided to create a companion for Altaira in the shape of a robot with female characteristics, including its voice, calling it Roberta. But it didn't work out. Altaira preferred to play with her friends the animals while Roberta goes off to sulk somewhere, thinking how beneath her Altaira is. "She knows nothing about sub-atomic particle declension," she'd say to herself, "not to mention quantum mechanics, all basic kid's stuff." And as for Morbius, she'd say, "I'm not a skivvy," and go away.

Now armed with more knowledge, Morbius created another Robot he called Robby. This one had male characteristics, was larger than Roberta and incorporated a small laboratory which enabled him to analyse and synthesize virtually anything.

He had a mild temperament too.

Now Morbius had an assistant but both Altaira and Roberta considered him theirs too. Poor Robby hardly had a minute to himself even though Morbius always had priority. Altaira would want him to create more clothes etc. for her, while Roberta always demanded her oil be perfumed on lube days. With her vast library of perfumes, she was able to come up with a different one each time which Robby had to make. Altaira liked this game too.

When the news of an approaching space ship came, also with the news that they were going to film Roberta's reaction was immediate. "They're not going to film me for people to gawk at and actors get paid. Money's no use to us." Which is why she doesn't appear in the film.

Robby, meanwhile, took refuge in one of his rare leisure moments, in what he called his comics. This was a huge collection of reproductions of mechanics magazines dating back 100 and more years. An exploded diagram of a Rolls Royce Merlin engine caused him to chuckle and he'd laugh out loud at the huge sprawl of an oil refinery. "How primitive," he'd say to Morbius, "I pity the people who had to live in the dark ages."

One thing Roberta could do which Robby couldn't was to change colour which she did according to her mood. She also refused to be photographed, keeping well away from the filming.

The Krell had left, among many other things, a large and complex maze using huge carved stones. One day Roberta got lost in it, her sense of direction not being too good. Altaira heard her cursing and saw her chance. She grabbed her camera and waited outside the exit. The camera was a small box with a cylindrical capsule inside which recorded the scene when a tiny shutter was opened, everything else was automatic. The capsule was inserted into a screen to view the scene.

At last Roberta emerged, bright red with rage. Altaira took the picture and scuttled off. There was nothing Roberta could do; both robots were programmed against harming any living thing.

The mysterious deaths being explained, it became imperative to not only leave the planet but to destroy it, the Krell having built a means of doing so into their vast machine. After consultation, it was decide to leave Roberta behind, she'd be too disruptive in the confines of the spaceship and there was no to time for Morbius to change her in any way. He, with reluctance, saw the wisdom of this and so it was done. Poor Roberta!

Back on earth, Robby was a great success going on to appear as a regular in the *Lost in Space* TV series while the one photograph of Roberta, which Altaira retains, is all that remains of her.

A Dream Come True

Charlie Winter loved the old castle that stood in all its grey majesty on a promontory about four miles from his home. It had stood thus for some 700 years, being added to from time to time then finally abandoned. It was at last tidied up by English Heritage, made safe where necessary and opened to the public.

As a child, Charlie's love of the castle became something of a joke to his parents and two elder sisters as he either drew pictures of it or re-read his local history book. They thought he'd grow out of it but no. As a teenager he visited it quite often, learned every one of its many nooks and crannies and became great friends with the curator, even acting as an unofficial guide in some cases.

Sometimes he would stand on the battlements and imagine he was Sir Charles de Winter, knight and lord of all he surveyed. He didn't fancy wearing armour though; it would be too heavy and hot.

He left school and went to work on the family farm which enabled him to feed and care for his own horse which in his mind was his faithful charger rather than ordinary old Nell.

One day there was great excitement in the village. A film was to be made in the castle and many extras would be required. The local newspaper gave details and Charlie phoned, the voice at the other end telling him to report to the castle the next week.

On the appointed day, he rode there on Nell and joined the crowd of other applicants, all of whom were taken on for various tasks.

A few days later the film crew arrived with lots of equipment and shouted orders as it was unloaded, set up and checked over.

Then the stars arrived. Tony Curtis and Janet Leigh no less, who were married to each other at the time. A crowd had gathered to see them arrive and at the sight of Janet a too-loud "Cor!" from one of the lads was rewarded with a steely glare from two large blue eyes. Charlie thought she was the most beautiful lady he'd ever seen. Tony just grinned and waved at everyone.

To his great delight, Charlie became one of the many soldiers needed. Among other things he was issued with a plastic set of chain mail, a surcoat emblazoned with a coat of arms, a wooden shield, a blunt sword with no edges made of some light alloy and a helmet made of the same alloy.

The soldiers weren't wanted every day but Charlie still went to watch. He managed for his father to photograph him with the two stars, both of whom kindly signed it when it was developed. The money extras were paid meant nothing to Charlie. In his mind, he was back in 1250, especially when he was in costume. He found it odd that scenes were not shot in sequence, not knowing that's how films are made. In the battle scenes, he wielded his sword with gusto.

There were two jousting scenes that would be carried out by stuntmen. While Tony Curtis would be seen at the start and finish, he was far too valuable to risk in the actual charges. But calamity! One of the stunt men went down with flu and delays were very expensive. There was also the ever-present threat of a change in the weather.

The director had noticed that Charlie rode a horse and in desperation asked him if he would take the stuntman's place. Just the charges, nothing more, the lances would be made of Styrofoam. Charlie couldn't believe his luck and practice started forthwith. Not on Nell, of course, but a large and very handsome stallion supplied by the film company.

On the day of the actual shooting, Charlie thought his heart would burst. There he was, the centre of attention and the full panoply of a medieval joust with the 'king' on his throne, the wonderful Janet Leigh and a large host of attendants, soldiers and spectators looking on plus Tony Curtis of course. The armour was a bit hot but, being made of a light alloy was not heavy.

The director required several takes and re-takes of the scene, shattered lances between each take cleared away between each take. Charlie didn't care, the more the merrier as far as he was concerned!

At last, the film was finished, the film crew and paraphernalia all packed away and the last vehicle departed.

Time marched on and in the fullness of time Charlie got married and had a family, carting them all off to the castle when the children were old enough or showing them the many photographs taken during the filming and the film itself of course.

The children grew up and left home and Charlie retired from work.

One day the position of castle curator was advertised. Charlie jumped at it and got it. Never was there a happier man!

Charlie had got 'his' castle at last and his wife was happy with their accommodation in it and the small tea room she ran.

They show the film on TV occasionally. It's called *The Black Shield of Falworth.*

A Big Turnaround

Victor didn't like foreigners. He didn't really know why and never thought deeply about it, prejudiced people never do. Foreign holidays were out of the question, and his wife, Hilary, had long since given up trying to change his mind.

But tonight he was a bit late. He and Hilary had arranged to meet at the local cinema to see the latest James Bond film, her office being near the cinema. Rushing as fast as the speed limit would allow, Victor noticed he needed fuel. "Oh hell," he said to himself, "I should have filled up this morning."

He pulled into the filling station which was thankfully empty, filled up, paid with his debit card then stuffed the card and receipt into his wallet which he returned to his back pocket – or so he thought.

At the cinema, he found Hilary pacing up and down. "You're late," she said accusingly.

"Sorry," he replied, "had to fill up." He went for his wallet to buy the tickets and, to his horror, discovered the pocket was empty! "I must have dropped it in the car," he said. The film forgotten, they rushed to the car but a good search of it proved fruitless. "The filling station then," said Victor, "let's hope it's been handed in."

But that proved fruitless too. The girl behind the counter said: "I did see a guy pick it up. I thought he'd dropped it and that it was his."

"What did he look like?" asked Victor, "did you get his car number?"

"I don't know his number," replied the girl. She went on: "He was foreign but spoke good English. Oh, he paid by card. Let me find his slip." She soon found it and it bore the name "H. Steiber."

"Huh," snorted Victor, "a bloody German. I won't see that again."

Sadly he drove home. Victor intended to cancel his debit and credit cards the next day. They didn't notice the Mercedes parked across the street.

They had hardly closed the front door when there was a knock on it. Surprised, Victor opened it to reveal a large blond man holding out his wallet!

The man said: “You are Mr Valton? I sink dis is yours.” For a moment, Victor was speechless. He took his wallet and said: “Thank you very much; I thought I’d seen the last of this. But why didn’t you just hand it in the filling station?”

“The responsibility vas mine,” answered the man, “it vas up to me to deal mit it as it vas me who found it.”

Again, Victor was struck by the man’s honesty and on an impulse said: “Would you like to come in?”

“Sank you,” came the reply, “my vife too? Ve are Hans and Lotte.”

“Of course,” piped up Hilary, “go and get her.”

So this was done. A meal was prepared and a bed offered for the night. Hans and Lotte gratefully accepted. They had to be up very early the next day to be on time for the Channel ferry, they were returning home after a holiday here.

Hilary could hardly believe the change in Victor. He and Hans chatted away about Brexit, the weather and all sorts of other things as if they’d known each other for years and Lotte’s English was even better than Hans’, her being an English teacher at Berlin University. A pleasant evening was had by all, with lots of good cheer.

Up to meet a rising sun and Hilary noted again the strangeness at breakfast with Victor entertaining the two Germans. They left with many thanks from both sides but it didn’t end there.

The next year found Hans and Lotte picking Victor and Hilary up from Templehof airport for a wonderful two weeks holiday.

Amazing, the effect a small act of kindness can have. Perhaps we should indulge in more of them!

Joe and the Seal

Joe loved sea fishing even though home and work commitments limited his sessions to one day each weekend, weather permitting, of course, although it had to be very bad to keep him indoors!

He'd found a nice secluded little bay where he could fish in peace. He'd got fed up with the usual places where others, invariably holidaymakers, would keep asking him questions such as: "Caught anything mate?" or "What's it like 'ere?" or "Anywhere else we can go?" The rubbish and beer cans they left annoyed him too.

But here he found peace. His catches were never huge, mostly dogfish which he always put back as they were hard to skin and he didn't like their flesh anyway. The occasional flounder, mackerel or even plaice, was a different matter and, providing they were large enough, he would gut them on the spot, putting the carcass into his cool box for later consumption by himself and his wife Dee Dee. The head, tail and entrails were soon cleared away by seagulls.

But one day a black, dog-like head appeared in the water. "Oh no," sighed Joe, "a blasted seal."

Sure enough, his catch, never large to begin with, dropped sharply. The seal even took fish from his line. Joe would shout at it to go away and even threw stones at it but the seal would simply swim out of range and bark annoyingly at him.

At home, he complained to Dee Dee who said, quite unsympathetically: "Go somewhere else then."

"I don't want to," retorted Joe, "it took me ages to find this place. Maybe the seal will go away."

But the seal didn't go away and Joe just had to put up with it even though it cast a damper on his enthusiasm.

One day, Joe went to the beach as usual and was tackling up when he spotted a dark shape near the water's edge. The seal? Dead? His problem solved? He quickly walked over to it and found the seal very much alive entangled in a piece of net, obviously from a boat. "Aha!" exclaimed Joe, "now I've got you," at the same time drawing his razor-sharp filleting knife from the sheath on his belt.

But how do you kill a seal? Stab it? Cut its throat? Joe hesitated as he looked at the creature which looked back of him. Suddenly a wave of compassion washed over as he realised there was no way he could end the seal's life. Instead, cursing himself – not very convincingly – for his sentimentality, he knelt down and cut the seal free.

Once released, it swam a few meters out to sea, apparently unharmed, then turned and barked twice "Arf! Arf!" as if to say "thank you."

"That's all very well!" shouted Joe, "but you keep pinching my fish!"

He gathered up the piece of net and dumped it next to his tackle box; he'd bin it at home later, then turned back to the business in hand.

He finished tackling up and cast out. But where was the seal? Then he spied it, right over to his left, by the rocks. A bite! Joe reeled it in, keeping one eye on the seal, but to his amazement it didn't move.

The fish was a dogfish and quite a good size. Joe unhooked it and was preparing to put it back when he thought of the seal. How long had it been caught in the net? Was it hungry? He walked to his left, the seal watching him.

"Here!" he shouted as he threw the fish. Both fish and seal hit the same bit of sea at the same time and the seal devoured the fish in one gulp.

So began an odd relationship. Joe would throw the fish he didn't want to the seal which, in return, never interfered with his fishing. Joe named it 'Sid' and would shout "Sid!" before he threw a fish, receiving an answering "Arf!" Obviously Sid had to fend for himself when Joe wasn't there.

One day, Sid didn't appear and it was the same thereafter. Something more than a year passed and with regret Joe thought he'd seen the last of him but no!

One day, Joe heard the familiar "Arf! Arf!" from his left and there was Sid! He walked over and three more black heads appeared, one a bit smaller than Sid's and the other two much smaller.

"So that's where you've been!" shouted Joe as all four seals began to bark. "You old rascal you!" The quartet ceased barking and swam as close as they could to him without getting stranded. He waded out to them as they lay quietly in the water, allowing him to pat and stroke each sleek head. A further wave of emotion swept over him as he realised these beautiful, helpless creatures trusted him absolutely not to hurt them and he was well aware of the filleting knife in its sheath dangling from his belt.

As if on a signal the four seals turned and swam out to sea, the adult female leading and Sid bringing up the rear. Joe stood transfixed, watching their bobbing heads growing smaller as they receded. One by one they vanished round the rocky point, but Sid turned and barked "Arf Arf!" before he too vanished.

The spell broken, Joe returned to his little stool and sat down feeling sad, wistful and nostalgic. He knew instinctively that he'd never see Sid again and that he'd just come back to show off his new family and once again say 'thank you' for saving his life.

Well, the sea's big enough for all of us, isn't it?

The End?

Hello!

I don't know why I'm bothering to write this. After all, there might not be anyone left to read it in a few weeks' time. But I like writing and I thought I should. Don't ask me why.

The moon is pretty close now and is due to hit us within the next few weeks.

Up until the year 2159, the moon was moving away from us causing the tides to become much lower. But then it stopped and started coming back. Something to do with the gravity of the sun and the earth changing, I believe.

We knew the earth would end someday so we needed to find another planet, but big problems. The distances in space are so vast that we use a light year to measure them. This is the distance light travels in a year which is about six billion (6,000,000,000,000) miles. Our own galaxy, which we call the Milky Way is about 100,000 light years across, so that's 100,000 X six billion miles which is a very large figure!

You couldn't travel at that speed, the acceleration would squash you like a fly. Rockets are far too slow.

Another problem is the time light takes to reach us. A famous galaxy is M31 which can be found in the constellation of Andromeda and is over two million light years away from us. This means when you look at it you're seeing it as it was over two million years ago instead of now, which is a bit of a nuisance.

Scientists realised a long time ago that it was time that was the problem, they needed to conquer that. Eventually they did it (don't ask me how) by finding another dimension where there is no time. They then constructed a Timescope, which is nothing like a normal telescope, and which we cannot see because it is in another dimension. What it sees is viewed on a screen.

They used the Timescope to look for another suitable planet, and at last they found one. This other planet, which they named Earth II, is 11,000 light years away, is slightly larger than our earth and has a similar atmosphere, plenty of water and vegetation, but no animals, rather like the earth as it was millions of years ago.

So next they made a Timecraft which works a bit like a projector and, due to problems in our atmosphere, floats in space, also in that other dimension so it can't be seen. Volunteers were then called for as this would be a one-way trip, no coming back. There were plenty of them and 50 were selected.

They got to Earth II in an instant where they were watched through the Timescope. They had no way of contacting us as radio signals travel at the same speed as light so a message would take 11,000 years to reach us. They did it using hand signals which indicated everything was fine. Maybe one day they'll construct their own Timecraft so they can communicate or come back here, assuming there's anything to come back to.

Then the moon started to return and the matter became urgent. Many people wanted to go but a surprising number didn't, including me, because at 84 years of age with no dependents, I'm not inclined to start again. Thousands of shuttles were built together with many more Timecraft and the great exodus began.

Animals up to the size of sheep were taken, plus insects, fish and birds. DNA of the larger animals and sea creatures was taken for cloning plus some of the contents of museums. Also thousands of chemical formulae, building techniques and instructions and plans for everything imaginable.

Meanwhile, we that are left await our fate.

The moon is calculated to hit the southern hemisphere. If it lands in the sea, it will cause enormous tidal waves, if on land it could knock the earth out of its orbit and blot out the sun with dust. The impact may well lift us off our feet only to fall down again with broken limbs or worse.

Things carry on pretty much as normal. There are still birds in the sky and there is still the odd airliner bringing refugees from the southern hemisphere. No more shuttles though, they're all grounded now.

So I'll see you around.

I hope.

Bye!

Serendipity

The 19-year-old twins Jessica and Sofia sat with their father Henry in the kitchen of their great-aunt Isabella's house. All looked tired and somewhat dishevelled.

"Well, that's it," said Henry. "We've searched absolutely everywhere."

Isabella had died a few weeks before, leaving everything to the two girls but 'everything' wasn't much at all as she seemed to have had no wealth.

"It's rather odd," went on Henry, "she used to say 'why spend your own money when you can borrow someone else's?' and didn't seem to care about the interest payable. She even sold this house to one of those companies that buy your house which becomes theirs when you die. Her will mentioned a box but we found nothing of any consequence in any box."

"Well, she was a nice old lady," said Jessica as Sofia nodded in agreement, "and was very generous to us at Christmas and on our birthdays."

"The house clearance guy is coming tomorrow," said Henry, "but I doubt if we'll get much for this lot, or her old car. We'll be lucky if we break a grand." After a pause, he went on: "The new owners want everything left to be cleared out so I've ordered a skip and a scaffolding plank for Saturday. We'll all have to muck in, your mum included, if we're to get it done in a day."

Saturday found the family hard at it. The girls cleared the house of old papers, magazines, books and other stuff the house clearance man didn't want while their mother, Ivy, hoovered after them. Henry, using Isabella's old wheelbarrow, wheeled loads of old tools, flower pots and broken tiles up the plank and into the skip to join the stuff the girls dumped.

At last, they were finished. The barrow was the last thing to go into the skip. As they turned to walk away Ivy noticed something. "The window box," she said, pointing, "I remember when Isabella had it bursting with flowers. Let's take it home. I can sand and repaint it. Come on Henry, give me a hand."

So they lifted it down and staggered to what was once a flower bed where they emptied it of dirt and weeds. Then the two girls carried it home.

The girls volunteered to do the sanding and the next day found them hard at it with various grades of sandpaper. At last, it was finished. "What about the base?" said Jessica. "Are we going to bother with that?"

"Might as well do the job properly," replied her sister.

They set to work, removing many layers of old paint. Then Sofia noticed something. "There are marks in the wood," she said. "Burn marks." The sanding continued to reveal two letters followed by a series of numbers. Henry was called to look.

"It could be an account number," he mused. "NW could stand for NatWest although there was nothing like that in the house." Then his mouth dropped open and he looked up. "Is this the box mentioned in the will? We'll check with the bank tomorrow." Ivy fetched pen and paper and Henry copied the number onto the paper.

The next morning found four excited people waiting at the door of their local NatWest bank. At last, it opened and they proceeded to the counter where Henry handed the paper to the cashier while the others looked on.

The cashier looked at the paper. "It's not an account number," she said, removing her spectacles. "It's a safe deposit box number. Please excuse me a moment." She went through a rear door marked 'Manager', emerging a few moments later to say, "Would you come through please."

She ushered them into the manager's office who held out the piece of paper, introduced himself as Mr Perkins and said: "where did you get this?" He looked from one to the other as they all chipped in with the tale of their discovery.

At last, they finished and Mr Perkins said: "I remember Mrs Isabella Lyman well. She came to her box at least once a year and always paid in cash. We always gave her receipts of course but from what you say she didn't retain them. Before I can hand the box over to you, I would need to see her death certificate, will and probate plus the birth certificates of the two girls."

The next day found Mr Perkins poring over the requested documents before four expectant faces. At last, he looked up. "All is in order," he said and produced two small keys from his desk drawer. "I had these ready," he went on, "Box number 119. Miss Tate will show you the way."

Henry thanked Mr Perkins and gathered the papers up from his desk. Then, together with Ivy and the girls, he followed Miss Tate to the vaults where she showed them where box 119 was then left them alone.

One of the keys opened the door to 119, the other one opened an oblong steel box they found inside which Henry placed on the table which stood in the middle of the room. Inside they found a large number of little tissue-paper parcels. Each one held either a gold sovereign or a piece of diamond jewellery. Four mouths fell open. “She must have been doing this for years,” said an amazed Ivy.

“Yes, and all for us,” said Jessica, tears rolling down her cheeks. Sofia cried too. Well twins always do things together, don’t they?

“She didn’t leave cash,” mused Henry, “probably because she knew cash devalues. She was very astute when it came to money.”

“Diamonds are forever,” said Sofia.

“So is gold,” added Jessica.

The sale of the box’s contents raised a goodly sum except for two of the sovereigns which the girls had mounted and wore on gold chains round their necks as a permanent reminder of their great-aunt Isabella.

So, another happy ending. Well we like those, don’t we?

A Fishy Tale

Mr Catfish and Miss Salmon sat together and enjoyed their champagne as they did every evening and had been doing for some nine months now. They discussed the events of the day and once more reminisced on their good fortune.

They had known each other for some two years and Mr Catfish felt himself very lucky as Miss Salmon had lots of admirers including Mr Starfish who gave her the best of the pearls he sometimes found inside the oysters he lived on.

They were also great friends with Mr and Mrs Turtle who were amphibious and were thus able to spend time out of the sea on the other world of dry land. Mr Catfish and Miss Salmon listened enthralled to their tales of life on the dry land although they found some of them a bit hard to swallow. "They ride about in boxes on round things they call wheels?" Queried Mr Catfish, "Why don't they walk on their legs?" Mr and Mrs Turtle didn't know. Mr Catfish and Miss Salmon knew what humans looked like, they'd seen them swimming in the shallow sea.

On dry land, Mr and Mrs Turtle had made the acquaintance of a certain Bill Doolittle who had the almost unique ability to be able to talk to animals. I say almost because he had a brother with the same ability, Dr Doolittle, was not only famous but had had a film made about him. Bill wanted none of this, only his wife Mary knew of his faculty.

Bill and Mary ran a small seaside restaurant which was very popular with holidaymakers in the summer and with locals all the year round. Mary's cooking was of the best.

Mr and Mrs Turtle told Bill about their friends Mr Catfish and Miss Salmon and Bill gave them a small bottle of champagne as a gift from him as well as some nice lettuce leaves for Mr and Mrs Turtle which they loved. Mr Catfish and Miss Salmon – especially Miss Salmon – greatly enjoyed the champagne. "I could have more of this," she said.

One day, as Mr and Mrs Turtle were enjoying their usual feed of lettuce in the restaurant kitchen they heard Mary say: “I do wish we could get some more prawns. That sauce I concocted would go so well with them. It’s a shame we have to use them all in the paella.”

Back in the sea the Turtles relayed this information to Mr Catfish and Miss Salmon. They looked at each other. “We know where there are loads of prawns,” said Miss Salmon, “you can hardly see the sea through them.”

“Ask Mr Doolittle for a net,” added Mr Catfish.

Mrs Doolittle supplied a piece of old net curtain and holding two corners each in their mouths Mr Catfish and Miss Salmon swam towards a huge shoal of prawns, the net billowing out behind them. Once through, they quickly swam together and tied the four corners together thus ensuring a good haul of prawns. Mr and Mrs Turtle helped get it into the shallows from where Bill Doolittle retrieved it.

Back at the restaurant Mary was thrilled. “Into the freezer with them,” she said. In due course, her prawn cocktail easily became the most popular starter on the menu.

So a deal was done. Regular supplies of prawns were exchanged for champagne. Bill even made chairs and a table for Mr Catfish and Miss Salmon and strung her pearls so she was able to wear them as a necklace. Fair exchange is no robbery!

So the next time you enjoy a prawn cocktail remember Mr Catfish, Miss Salmon, Mr & Mrs Turtle, Mr Starfish and Bill & Mary Doolittle. But please, don’t try to find them – they don’t exist!

Beryl's Lot

Beryl boarded the bus that would take her to the auction which she had been doing for longer than she could remember. It was the same every month, the last Wednesday in the month was viewing day, the sale itself the next day. Not that Beryl ever bid for anything, her pension didn't stretch to that and it was only her free bus pass that enabled her to attend at all.

Over the years the auctioneer, Simon had noticed her regular attendance and spoke to her. "I love coming here," she had said, "it's so different each month, a bit like a museum that keeps changing its display. I can't afford to bid for anything but I don't mind." Simon then got into the habit of giving her a £2 catalogue each month.

Beryl would spend a good two hours looking at all the lots then she would return home to study all the entries in the catalogue.

The next day would find her back again, nice and early to be sure of a seat and equipped with a flask and sandwiches. As the auction progressed she would write down the price realised against each item in her catalogue. She thus became quite proficient at valuing things herself.

Back home at the end of the day, she would settle herself in her armchair with a bit of supper and go through the catalogue again. "She got a bargain there," she might say to herself, or: "He paid far too much for that," or again: "They must have been mad buying that; I wouldn't give it house room."

While the monthly auction was the highlight of Beryl's otherwise humdrum life, particularly bad weather would keep her at home, but one auction day caught her out. The morning was cold and overcast but dry so Beryl decided to risk it. But as the morning wore on the sky darkened and freezing sleet began to fall. After the auction finished, Beryl stood in the doorway hoping the weather would clear before her walk to the bus stop. Simon spotted her leaning on her stick waiting and said to his assistant: "Keep an eye on things, I'm popping out." Then to Beryl: "Come on, love, I'll give you a lift, you can't hang about in this."

It was cold in Simon's car but much better than being outside. "Thank you very much," said Beryl as they reached her flat, "would you like a cup of tea?" "I sure would," replied Simon, "all that talking at the auction, it would be very welcome."

They entered her flat and passed into the living room. Simon sat down then quickly jumped up, saying: "No, it can't be." On a shelf, he'd noticed three Staffordshire dogs.

Staffordshire dogs were always made in pairs of porcelain and were modelled on seated spaniels. Mirror images of each other they sat and stared out at the world with impassive faces. Very popular in their heyday, they graced each end of many a Victorian or Edwardian mantelpiece. These days they were very much out of favour and fetched only low prices.

The three that Beryl had were all odd ones, their companions having been lost or, much more likely, broken. Usually odd ones were thrown away but Beryl had found two of hers at jumbles sales and the other one in a charity shop. She'd had them for many years, none of them costing more than 50p. She had become quite attached them and called them, "Pip, Squeak and Wilfred" after 'Daily Mirror' cartoon characters she remembered from long ago.

Now, Simon carefully picked up 'Wilfred' and turned him over, gasping when he saw a script C.P. on the underside. "This one is from Chiltern Potteries," he said and went on: "Joseph Chiltern made them as a spoof, a dog's body with human eyes and a cat's face. He only made a few before he died suddenly and nobody liked them anyway. The only other place I've seen them is in the Victoria and Albert museum."

"Well I never," said Beryl. "Is he worth anything?"

"He certainly is," replied an excited Simon. "Collectors would fight over it. Let me auction it for you. You would be able to come to the auction in a taxi in future instead of having to wait around for buses."

And so it was arranged. Simon took 'Wilfred' away with him and a few days before the auction Beryl received a complimentary catalogue by post featuring 'Wilfred' on the cover in full colour.

She went to the viewing as usual. Wilfred was in a locked glass case, apart from the other auction items. She had given no thought to 'Pip and Squeak' or little else in her excitement but now, as she saw 'Wilfred' all alone in his case, she felt a qualm.

Back home, she gazed at the other two and 'Wilfred's' space. Suddenly a feeling of dread came over her. "I can't do it," she said to herself. "Simon will be disappointed but it can't be helped."

After a restless night, she got her usual bus to the auction, which was more crowded than usual. She gave Simon the bad news, that 'Wilfred' would have to be withdrawn from the sale. He blanched but could see that Beryl was not to be moved so reluctantly announced it over the microphone. There was an audible groan from the audience and several people, probably dealers, left.

Beryl stayed until the end of the auction which still went well even without 'Wilfred' owing to the larger than usual audience. At the end, Simon called her a taxi. "You can't take that on a bus," he said, "don't worry, I'll pay for it."

Back home Beryl put 'Wilfred' back in his place, made her supper and settled in her chair. She looked at her three mute friends and could have sworn 'Wilfred' winked at her. "'Pip, Squeak and Wilfred' and me," she said aloud, "the gang's all here!"

Well, some things are worth more than money, aren't they?

Tomorrow Never Comes

The biggest problem was Max. He was a two-year-old Great Dane and was big, heavy and full of life. His domain was the large front garden with its high wall and 'Beware of the dog' sign on the gate. Max was not vicious, on the contrary he was over friendly and his habit of jumping up could push an adult over if he or she was caught unawares. A child didn't stand a chance.

The house was semi-detached, the home of Greg and Olive Pitman. They were both retired and their married daughter, son-in-law and three grandchildren lived next door. They both had hobbies. Olive's was baking. For her every day was baking day and her efforts, all of which were very good, were much appreciated by the family next door. Mary Berry was akin to a god in Olive's eyes and she had a good collection of cookery books and handed-down recipes.

Greg was a ham radio enthusiast. After much reading, head-scratching and end of pen biting he passed the exam set by the Radio Society of Great Britain with flying colours and was currently learning morse code on a horizontal key which was operated from side to side by a thumb and forefinger, a much faster method than the old vertical key. He also loved talking to people all over the world.

In the back garden was his aerial, a complex array of elements at the top of a tall wooden pole. Being top-heavy, guy ropes anchored the pole upright; all after planning permission had been obtained.

Exterior access to the back garden was via a gate fixed between the house and boundary walls. It was a bit rickety as the screws that held the hasp post to the boundary wall were a bit loose. Greg's rejoinders to Olive's continual reminders to fix the post were: "No hurry, Max can't undo the lock; I'll look at it tomorrow." But he was so engrossed in his morse code that he kept putting it off.

Friday was, as usual, shopping day, which had to be done despite a very strong wind. While Greg and Olive were slowly making their way around Tesco's aisles the wind grew stronger. Max just dozed in his kennel.

Then a very strong gust was followed by a crash which caused Max to perk up and go out to investigate. The wind had blown the gate open, tearing the screws and wall plugs out of the boundary wall and slamming it, complete with hasp post, against the house wall. Naturally, Max entered the back garden.

Once there he looked around and soon spied the guy ropes as things to play with. Grabbing one in his teeth, he shook his powerful head and growled, causing its peg to come out of the ground. Other ropes were treated in the same way, much to Max's satisfaction. The wind was still very strong and the top-heavy pole, no longer supported by the guy ropes, snapped, allowing the elements to fall onto the boundary wall which bent or broke nearly all of them. This made Max jump so he retreated to his kennel and dozed anew.

Greg and Olive were thus confronted with the wreck when they returned home. Max's paw prints and teeth marks told their own story. "I told you to fix that gate!" scolded Olive, "I knew I should have asked Sam to do it." Greg surveyed the wreck of his aerial. No more radio ham for him or learning morse code until he'd erected another aerial at considerable expense and re-fixed the hasp post, strongly this time.

So, before you put off a task until tomorrow remember: tomorrow never comes.

Temple of Doom

The three men sat in the chiefs hut, solemn looks on their faces. "The crops are not good again," said the chief, "and two more goats have died."

"The Gods are not happy with us," rejoined the head priest. "I have prayed, made sacrifice and many incantations but to no avail. They have turned their faces away from us."

"Perhaps we should all move," said the wise man.

"There's no point," replied the head priest, "their displeasure would just follow us."

The chief became exasperated: "Well, we must do something!" He shouted.

The wise man then spoke again: "I have travelled far and wide and seen many things," he said in an authoritative tone; "other tribes have given up outdoor worship in favour of very large huts they call 'temples'. I suggest we do the same as they all seem to prosper."

The head priest jumped up excitedly. "That's it!" he cried, "and as you've seen these temples you could design one!"

The chief concurred. "Ours must be the biggest and best one. The Gods must be placated."

And so it began. Huge stone blocks were quarried and the wise men told them of other, different stone he'd seen in the land next to The Big Water. "We must have some," he pronounced, "I believe it to be magic."

So a large number of people travelled to the land next to The Big Water and marvelled at the stone which they quarried and transported, partly by sea on rafts and partly overland on rollers made from logs.

Such a huge undertaking could not be completed in one generation so succeeding ones carried on what had been started. At last, the temple neared completion.

It was a circle of huge oblong stones topped by others which were fixed by mortise and tenon joints. Inside was a horseshoe and altar made of magic stone brought from the land next to The Big Water. Concentric rings of smaller stones surrounded the whole thing together with a large ditch and bank. The gaps between the large stones were filled with intertwined branches forming walls and the roof was made in the same way, supported by rafters made of thick branches. An avenue with a bank on each side led to the main entrance. An opening ceremony was arranged to take place on seven suns hence.

Gaj and Hekka were brothers, twins in fact. Gaj liked to play with his mates having, among other things, races, stone and spear-throwing competitions and a game they called 'ball-foot' in which they kicked a ball about made of rabbit skins tied with leather thongs.

Hekka on the other hand was much more studious and spent his days wandering about examining and noting everything he saw. One day, while their parents were away helping to put the finishing touches to the temple, he called Gaj over to him. "Watch this," he said.

Gaj saw he had three small piles of powder. He recognised the black one as charcoal but the yellow and white ones were new to him. Hekka mixed some from each of the piles. "Took me ages to get this right," he said. He then got a burning stick from the fire and applied it to his little heap. Immediately there was a 'pfft' and a brief flash of bright flame which made Gaj jump.

"Wow!" he exclaimed, "That's fantastic!"

"I call it 'fire dust'," said Hekka, "and I want your help with an idea. I want to put a big lot of fire dust in the temple secretly then light it as the opening ceremony begins. This will make a big light which will amaze everybody and please the Gods." Gaj enthusiastically agreed.

So a large amount of the fire dust was made which the boys stacked in the empty temple the night before the opening ceremony. They used the back entrance; only the chief, the priests and the wise men were allowed to use the grand front entrance with its avenue. They laid a trail of fire dust back to two of the outer stones, behind which they secreted themselves the next morning.

By the time of the first glow of sunrise, a large crowd was gathered each side of the avenue. Then the sun rose and the slow, solemn procession started, the head priest making loud prayers to the sky. "Now," said Gaj.

Hekka blew on the smoking stick he was holding and applied it to the fire dust trail. A small light then ran along it. What the brothers couldn't know of course was that it was not a good idea to light fire dust, especially a large quantity, in a confined space. The little light disappeared into the temple whereupon there was a very loud WHUMPF! And a fierce blast which lifted the roof and blew out the walls. The roof collapsed and all of them burst into flames. Some of the stones were dislodged to lean drunkenly while others fell down.

The men on the avenue were blown flat on their backs while those in the crowd all threw themselves to the ground on terror; many began to wail.

The head priest was the first to regain his feet and he cried: “We’ve failed! The Gods have shown their anger! We must all leave here!”

The two boys, deeply shocked, crept back to their beds. “Not a word to anyone,” ordered Hekka.

The next day everyone packed up and left the area for new pastures. One hopes their fortunes improved. The temple ruins can still be seen today, we call them Stonehenge.

There was no more fire dust. Hekka learnt to play ball-foot and the secret died with him only to be re-discovered 2,000 years later, reputedly by the Chinese. We call it gunpowder.

Art at the Beginning

Groz entered the cave where he lived with his wife, Kal, and their son Graf. He leant his flint tipped spear against the wall and noted the simmering clay pot on the semi-circle of stones with a good fire beneath. "I'm home," he called and Kal came in from a side chamber. Groz gave her the two deceased rabbits he was carrying.

"Not bad," she said, taking them, then: "Urrg's gone off again. I just can't watch him all day."

"Oh no," said Groz wearily, "I'm just too tired to go looking for him; Graf will have to do it."

"He's in his room," replied Kal with a stern look on her face. "He's been drawing on his walls again and he upset his class at school today by asking for history when he knows there isn't any yet."

The age of the dinosaurs had passed but a few of the smaller ones had survived. People tended to keep them as pets as they kept rats and lizards away. Urgg was the family pet. He would sometimes wander away in the daytime and his grey skin made him very hard to spot in the thick undergrowth. Another area presented the same problem. It was strewn with a mass of grey boulders and Urgg liked nothing better than leaning up against one which had been warmed by the sun and dozing as dinosaurs slept standing up.

As for humans, their language was quite well developed by then although they still didn't have names for some things. Most of their words have become lost to us over time although 'itti' their word for 'stop' has been passed down. When Grafs mother caught him drawing on his wall she would say, "Graf! Itti!" which we still use to describe amateur wall paintings today, rendered with aerosol cans rather than brushes.

Groz went to get his son who was glad to get out into the fresh air and quickly ran off to find Urgg. Groz stood for a while looking at his drawings and the little clay pots he kept his colours in.

By and by, Graf returned with Urgg, by which time the rabbits and wild vegetables, which they didn't yet have names for, were cooked. As they ate Groz remained dead in thought. Finally he said: "Graf, how do you make those colours?"

"Easy, Dad," replied his son. "I get grass, leaves, berries and flowers and boil them one at a time until the water turns the same colour. Then I let it cool, remove the grass or whatever and mix clay in the water to make a paste."

"I see," mused Grog. "I've got an idea. Can you make a lot of each colour? No, it's not for drawing on walls," he added hastily as Kal glared at him.

"Okay, Dad," said Graf cheerfully. "It's too dark now. I'll do it tomorrow."

And so the next day it was done. That evening when Urgg was fast asleep, and working from burning grass torches, Groz and Graf painted him with grass brushes in bright, garish, colours. He never got lost again, being easy to spot wherever he was.

As for Groz, he looked again at Grafs drawings. "They're pretty realistic," he said to himself, feeling rather proud of his son's ingenuity and skill "I wonder if I could do it?"

And that, dear friends, was the beginning of what we call art.

Take Flight

Rodney Burke had one great interest in life: aeroplanes and flight. As far back as he could remember, he had read everything he could get hold of on the subject either via his local library or what magazines his meagre pocket money would allow. Christmas and birthday presents were mostly flight related, maybe a book or a model kit, which he would carefully construct and display on any flat surface he could find in his room.

His one ambition was to learn to fly but with lessons costing £70 per hour, way beyond the means of his parents and his paper round earnings, it remained a dream. But the yearning grew more insistent as he grew.

When he was fourteen, he conceived the idea of using his old soap box cart, built by his father in the form of a racing car, and a ramp to launch himself into the air. He put the idea to his father who thought him mad. "But Dad," said Rodney, "I could land on cardboard boxes like stuntmen do in films." After a lot more persuasion, his father gradually came round to the idea.

His mother, however, did not. "Don't come running to me if you break your neck," she said with that irrefutable logic all mothers have as with a broken neck Rodney wouldn't be running anywhere.

So the cart, which hadn't been used for years, was hauled out from the back of the shed, cleaned up and had its axles well-greased. The ramp, with take-off section, looked like a giant hockey stick and featured channels for the wheels to run in to prevent Rodney from ignominiously tumbling off sideways. A large assortment of cardboard boxes was assembled.

At last, the great day came and, wearing his father's old crash helmet, Rodney achieved his dream. Well, sort of. Mr Burke filmed the whole thing on his camcorder.

It all worked well – too well. Rodney sailed right over the cardboard boxes and landed in the ditch beyond. His father rushed to his aid, leaving the camcorder running on its tripod, but collapsed with laughter as a figure, apparently made of black mud, arose from the ditch with two white eyes and a spluttering mouth uttering sounds of distress.

After getting cleaned up, Rodney sat with his parents to watch the camcorder footage on their television. His mother saw the funny side but with the firm admonition that the 'flight' would not be repeated.

On a whim, Mr Burke sent the tape to the *You've Been Framed* television programme with a letter of explanation. Some weeks passed then he and Rodney were surprised when a cheque for £750 arrived, £250 for the tape plus £500 for it being adjudged as that weeks' best. The family watched it on the television with delight. Someone else did too.

Two weeks later another letter arrived which contained an envelope. A covering letter said:

Dear Rodney,

The enclosed letter was sent to us following our showing of your tape on the 8th Inst.

We have vetted the sender and he is genuine.

Once again, thank you for your contribution.

Signed: "Julie Wainwright, producer You've Been Framed*."*

The writing on the envelope was to reveal another letter on better quality note paper and with an address and phone number embossed at its opened head. It read:

Dear Sir,

I do hope you will excuse me for writing to you but I was inspired to when I saw you during the You've Been Framed *TV programme.*

I lost my wife four years ago and my life has been rather empty since but when I saw you emerge from that ditch I laughed in a way I hadn't done for years.

I note your desire to learn to fly and as I have my own aircraft I am in a position to assist you which would give me some purpose in life.

Please contact me on the above number if you are interested and please show this letter to your parents.

I look forward to hearing from you.

Signed: "David J. Williams."

Rodney couldn't get to the phone quickly enough. Mr Williams answered and soon became acquainted with Rodney and his dream. A visit was arranged which culminated with Rodney and his parents soaring aloft in Mr Williams' four-seater, twin-engine Beechcraft aeroplane, Rodney in the co-pilots seat of course. He knew what most of the controls were, throttles, altimeter, artificial horizon, turn and bank indicator, pitch and yaw indicator etc. Mr Williams then said to Rodney: "Hold the wheel and keep it still, also the rudder bar with your feet on it." Rodney obeyed whereupon Mr Williams continued: "I'm letting go now so you have control."

Rodney's exhilaration knew no bounds, he was flying!

The visit was followed by many more and when Rodney was at last old enough to go for his pilot's license he didn't need many lessons, insisting on using his £750 to pay for them.

These days he flies airlines for British Airways, a framed example of a picture of him 'flying' in his soap box cart always hanging somewhere in his cockpit.

The Biter Bit

Jeff Colson sat in his dressing gown waiting for his phone to ring. He was outside on the patio of his luxury house which, together with five others, comprised an exclusive gated community, fenced all round and with 24-hour security.

The houses stood on a cliff overlooking a deserted sandy beach, a zig zag path leading down (or up if you were on the beach) from one to the other. On any other day Jeff, owner of Colson Mining, would run down the path, along the beach, and back again and all before breakfast cooked by Kate, his latest girlfriend, who he could hear bustling about in the kitchen.

At last, the phone rang and Jeff snatched it up. It was Mike, his works manager. "Well?" asked Jeff without any preliminaries.

"We've got it," replied Mike. "Jennings will finalise the contracts today and I'll be flying out tomorrow."

"Great," said Jeff, "I'll join you in two weeks."

Colson Mining specialised in the mining of natural ores in poor countries that could not afford to do it themselves. Finance was provided by an American company and the invariably huge profits were split three ways, Colson, the Americans and the country concerned. How much of the latter went into the Swiss bank accounts of corrupt officials was no concern of Jeff's. In fact, that was how he got some of his contracts.

Kate came out carrying two plates. She set them down and they both ate in silence. When she took the plates and cutlery away and returned with coffee and toast, Jeff spoke: "I'm going to have to go away," he said.

"Oh? Where?" Came the reply.

"Africa," he said casually.

Kate raised her eyebrows in surprise. "Africa? How long for?"

"Two years or so," he replied. "Just landed a big contract there, copper, you can come if you like."

Kate jumped up. "Two years on a building site?" she said angrily. "All dust and noise and nothing to do? No fear, and I'm not staying here on my own either!"

And so it was the parting of the ways for Jeff and Kate. He wasn't unduly bothered. Plenty more where she came from and he never stayed long with anyone anyway. Very egotistical was Jeff.

Two weeks later found him at the site, where portacabins had been erected, talking to Mike. "The usual problem," Mike was saying. "The natives don't like it. Apparently the site is underneath land they've farmed for generations and there isn't much land like that around here."

"Tough," said Jeff, "We have license from their government and you can't stop progress."

"Well, some of them are coming to see you," said Mike. "I tried to put them off but it was no good, they depend on the land for food."

"We'll employ them in the mine so they'll be able to buy their food." Rejoined Jeff. "Don't pay them too much though, they'll only get drunk!"

The delegation duly arrived with their grievances. "Make it short, will you?" was how Jeff greeted them, "I'm jetlagged." So they repeated what Mike had said although in considerable more detail. At last, Jeff said: "Look, you can't stop progress. The world needs copper and did you know that America used to be the world's largest exporter of copper? Now they're the world's largest importer and have been for at least fifty years."

In vain did the delegation protest. "You can't stop progress," was Jeffs answer to each of their objections, "we'll employ you all in the mine and pay you."

"We doan wanna work in no mine," came the answer, "we like outside."

"You will be outside," replied Jeff wearily. "It will be an open cast mine – a big hole in the ground."

The delegates were aghast. Their fields replaced by a big hole? Eventually they left, despondent.

Nearly two years passed. It takes a long time to get a huge mine up and running and Jeff could now return home, leaving Mike to run things. He phoned his housekeeper asking her to open up the house and get some food in as he'd be home in two days' time.

Back home at last, Jeff entered his house, empty without Kate but "oh well," he sighed resignedly. Mrs Burke had filled the fridge and freezer, leaving the bill neatly pinned to the kitchen notice board and leaving a couple of windows open.

Jeff opened the patio doors and stepped out. A faint sound caught his ears. "Sounds like a boat," he said to himself. He stepped to the end of the lawned garden and looked over the drop. His eyes widened in horror. Instead of his lovely deserted beach he saw buildings, caravans, motor homes, the water filled with small boats and jet skis and lots of people scuttling about!

He went next door, the house was empty. Puzzled, Jeff went to the house on the other side of his. His friend, Henry, opened the door.

"Hello Jeff," he said, "you're back then?"

"What the hell has happened to the beach?" said Jeff, ignoring the greeting.

"It's now a designated leisure area," replied Henry. "The council gave planning permission just after you left without any public consultation. It's really knocked the value of our houses. Terry and Ruth left six weeks ago but have not been able to sell and the guy at the end is the same. I would have gone too but Becky won't move."

"Oh my God," exclaimed Jeff, "what a disaster!" Then: "What can we do about it?"

"Nothing," said Henry ruefully. "It's like you always say: 'You can't stop progress!'"

Improvisation

The family that moved into Homelea farm were odd to say the least. Even the farm was a shadow of what it once was, its original size having been greatly reduced by the sale of various fields over the years. Now it was just the house, a large shed, a couple of rickety stables and a small field used as a paddock for the family's one horse. They were just four in number, Mr & Mrs Jones, Brian, a strapping lad of eighteen and his little sister Jess, aged three. They existed by doing odd jobs for people, either in their own homes or in the shed which served as a workshop. A bit of dealing in scrap metal didn't go amiss either and Mrs Jones did one or two cleaning jobs as well as doing folks' washing at the same time. Mr Jones could turn his hand to almost anything. "Prune yer roses for yer missus," he'd say or things like: "That wall needs pointing mate, yer don't want the rain to get through. Sort it for yer if yer likes." Broken bicycles were mended in the shed along with many other things and Brian was always there, learning his father's many skills.

A cart for the horse was kept in the shed and that, plus the horse, was the family's sole means of transport which looked very out of place among the cars in Tesco's car park when the family did their weekly shop.

The family didn't just live in what might well be considered an old fashioned way, they dressed like it, the two men with red neckerchiefs, plain waistcoats, leather belts with large brass buckles all topped off with a bowler hat for father and a trilby for son. Mother always wore a long, ankle length dress which buttoned up to the neck and favouring a bonnet as her crowning glory. Little Jess was a miniature of her mother, looking more like a doll than a little girl.

Questions as to their way of life were answered with a stern glare and: "It's jest the way we prefers things, see?" which effectively shut the questioner up. Apart from that and generally keeping themselves to themselves the Jones' were friendly enough and soon became accepted by the community.

One day, the people were amazed to see the diminutive Jess perched on a four-wheeled cart pulled by an alligator! Parents pulled their children back and dogs growled but instinctively kept well away from the fearsome-looking beast even though it was muzzled.

The local newspaper was contacted and a reporter and photographer soon came. The resultant photo and article duly appeared to the wonder and amusement of the local populace accompanied by a gratifying increase in papers sold.

Mr Jones had said: “Young Jess wanted a pony like but we didn’t ’ave the money fer one, see? So I bought a baby ’gator and raised it in the stable with the ’orse, feedin’ it oats and stuff. So now it thinks it’s an ’orse. Make do and mend, see?”

A Small Bit

Stanley owned a very rare veteran motor-cycle – a Wilkinson. He'd owned it for many years and had bought it from the son of the original owner. While complete, it had been in something of a sorry state, not having been ridden, or even started, for many years.

The bike was very advanced for its time being shaft-driven with three gears behind a four-cylinder engine and was only made between 1909 and 1916 when Wilkinson had turned to the war effort making swords, knives and bayonets and then at the cessation of hostilities turning to garden tools, which they still make today.

Stanley was very lucky to be given the original maintenance book by the seller. He photocopied it, using the copy as reference. This was well-thumbed as Stanley, over a great many months, carefully stripped the bike, thoroughly cleaned it and replaced some parts such as the spark plugs and carburettor diaphragm, all of which the Veteran Motor-cycle Owner's Club was able to supply as these parts were common to other bikes from the same era. Nothing major needed replacing although the re-chrome plating of the wheels and the exhaust pipe was necessary. Apart from new tyres, also supplied by the owner's club, this was Stanley's largest expense.

There was nothing metric on the bike, of course, so Stanley's toolbox was full of spanners from the pre-metric area viz. BSF, AF, Whitworth etc. He never touched his car in that way, he left that to the garage, but no one touched his beloved Wilkinson, which he only rode on sunny, dry days.

But today Stanley was despondent. The bike wouldn't start! Tomorrow was the day of the annual Veteran Motor-cycle Rally which was held about 40 miles from where he lived. A nice inscribed trophy was awarded to the owner of the bike which the judges deemed to be the best turned out. It now sat in pride of place on Stanley's mantelpiece as he'd won it for the past two years. No longer confident of making it a hat-trick he would now have to attend in his car to return the trophy, then slink away to avoid the smirks and sarky comments of the other contestants, especially from the one who'd won the trophy.

To prepare for the event Stanley had spent a whole weekend cleaning and checking his bike, gapping the spark plugs and stripping and cleaning the carburettor as just one speck of grit could ruin his day.

Now, after much frantic head scratching, he'd found the problem. The carburettor needle was missing, causing the engine to constantly flood. Stanley searched high and low, his workbench, the floor on hands and knees with a torch and a magnet and his toolbox, but to no avail.

A trip in the car to the nearest large dealer was in vain. None of the staff had heard of a Wilkinson and none of their stock of needles was anything like the missing one. The afternoon found a despondent Stanley sat gloomily in his old armchair. Neither his wife not his friend from next door, Harry, could cheer him up.

Then the door opened and in came his granddaughter, a precocious little tyrant at three years old, followed by her parents. Stanley's face lit up, she never failed to cheer him. "Hello Sally," he said, "Give us a cuddle."

"Hello, Granddad," she replied. "Can you get up please? I want to go treasure hunting."

Mystified, Stanley stood up whereupon she dived on to his chair and plunged her arm down behind the cushion. "She does this at home," said her mother. After a few seconds, the arm emerged clutching a 10p coin. "Treasure!" squealed the little girl. Down went the arm again but when it emerged this time Sally looked puzzled. "What's this, Granddad?" she said. Stanley gasped: "It's my carb needle! I must have put it in my pocket without thinking when I stopped for lunch while stripping the carb!"

"Come on, Stan," said Harry, "I'll get your tools." The needle was soon replaced and the Wilkinson running as sweetly as it had ever done.

The next day the only smirk was on Stanley's face as he rode home from the rally, his wife and Harry following in the car, Harry holding the trophy!

The Solution

Yet again James sat on the seat he'd placed at the foot of the steps to his little cottage as he'd been doing every Saturday evening for months. He was well wrapped up against the weather. Even though the January snow was turning to slush, it was still bitterly cold. The Cheshire cat grin of the crescent moon shone forth from a cloudless sky, offering the promise of a hard frost on the morrow.

James had bought his cottage three years previously after satisfying himself that the noise from the nearby community centre would either be non-existent or lower than the volume of his radio which he listened to nearly all the time. He shunned television, computers and suchlike, no unsightly aerials or dishes on his house! His only concession to modern living was the installation of a hot water and central heating system powered by electricity. He'd paid for the fireplaces to be blocked up and the chimneys removed.

For two-and-a-half years, things had been fine. The pre-school play group and W.l. gatherings rarely made enough noise to be heard outside the confines of the community centre. Then, six months ago, the council, always looking to increase its income, had agreed to hire the centre out for Saturday night dances, the music being provided either by a disco or a live group.

Of course there was opposition; by far the most vociferous of them coming from James but to no avail, the increased income triumphed over the dissenting voices.

The subsequent dances had been a great success to everybody except James; local bands, to James' ears, seemed to be more concerned with volume than anything melodic but, to judge by the constant good attendances by the local youth and a few not so young, he was in a minority of one.

James had decided to carry out his own one-man protest. Every Saturday evening, he sat outside his cottage and glowered at the occupants of cars as they arrived. They soon got used to that and would either ignore him or jeer whereupon James would shout: “Go home!” or “Go away!” and shake his fists at them.

This night promised to be no different. The caretaker had arrived some time ago to turn on the lights and heating and it wouldn’t be too long before other vehicles started to arrive. First would come the band’s van then a parade of cars, their occupants looking forward to a good Saturday night out. But there was something else coming.

As James sat staring gloomily at the slushy, rutted road he was unaware of another object in the sky, one that was rapidly approaching the very spot where he sat.

This was a meteorite which was too large to burn up by atmospheric friction but too small to be detected by sky watchers until it was too close.

Had James been indoors with his radio on, he would have heard the frantic warnings of the announcer.

Between them the meteorite and gravity caused a terrific explosion that wiped out James’ cottage and the community centre, permanently removing James and the caretaker from this earthly existence.

Neither the cottage nor the community centre was re-built. The whole episode was regarded as a bad omen. A new centre was built some distance away.

A Lonely Life

The road was a lonely one being little used and not in a particularly good condition. This suited Albert just fine as he ambled along. After all, he wasn't going anywhere special. He never was, being what so-called ordinary folk would regard as a tramp.

Albert felt quite refreshed after a night spent in a haystack and a quick swill in an ice-cold stream brought him to life as it were. The last of his bread and cheese, donated by a kindly farmer's wife and complemented by an apple from her tree, had provided his breakfast before he set off once more on any road to any place where he would never stay long.

Albert's antecedents were obscure. He'd grown up in a hated orphanage where a combination of harsh treatment and bullying had caused him to retreat even further into himself, developing a great love of the countryside and the wildlife in it rather than people. When he became old enough to leave he did so, leaving the world of people, towns, traffic, mortgages and all the other appurtences of modern living as far behind him as possible.

It was not that he actually disliked people as he was able to survive due to a combination of their generosity and what decent folk would call scavenging, with payment for the occasional job thrown in. Not for him a bed in a room, his bed was the living earth, his blanket the sky – unless it was raining of course and there was always a barn somewhere in the winter.

Now he strolled along, grinning at the crows which flew off squawking at his approach and noted a squirrel which paused to stare at him before scampering up a tree. Then he saw something through the trees, a tip!

A few steps further brought him to a track which led to the tip. Albert reached it and looked at it with a practiced eye; he was quite an expert on tips. In fact, all his clothes had come from them except his trainers which he'd bought from money earned. *A small village tip*, he thought, *I won't find much here*.

More in hope than expectation he began to rummage around but after an hour had found nothing of note. Then he felt the handle of something and pulled it out. An old cricket bat! "I might get a quid or two for it," he thought. Then he noticed something, it had signatures on it. Knowing nothing about cricket anyway, Albert didn't recognise any of them although one 'Bradman' did ring a very faint bell.

Rather than detour around the next town, Albert went into it and found a sports shop. The owner gasped when he saw the bat. "This has been missing for years," he said, and went on: "Donald Bradman was visiting relatives here and played a friendly match with a local village team and they all signed the bat." "Oh," said Albert, absentmindedly rubbing his chin, "is it worth anything?" "Well, I'm sure there'll be a good reward," replied the shopkeeper. "It must have been accidently thrown out and not stolen as folks thought."

And so it was. The bat, after eventual judicious cleaning, was accorded place of honour in a glass case in the local village hall when it was admired by all. And Albert? He was the hero of the hour and the reward was indeed generous. Many were the offers of bed and board – free of course – but Albert politely declined them all. "Thank you but I must be getting along," he said. Time was getting along and he needed to find another haystack!

A Near Thing

Private Jim Billings awoke with a start. For a few moments, he had to think about where he was. The sun was up and its light came streaming through a tiny window. His watch read 5:22 a.m.

It the far distance he could hear the sound of gunfire. "Oh hell," he exclaimed. "I'd better shift myself, the Jerries will be here sooner than I'd like." He'd well overslept.

The year was 1944 and, although the Germans were being slowly and inexorably forced into defeat, there was plenty of fight left in them yet. Jim's infantry unit had somehow got lost and found itself in danger of being overrun by superior enemy forces equipped with tanks. An escape route lay along a nearby river but that would be closed before too long. In the resultant confusion, Jim had become separated from his unit which was at that time a long way ahead of the Germans.

Hungry and nearly exhausted after much tramping over the flat fields of Holland Jim had come across a deserted windmill, just the place for a kip out of the rain. The door was not locked and there were signs such as sacks of flour that the mill had had recent use. Maybe the owners had fled until the war had passed them by.

A field of carrots lay nearby. Jim pulled a couple and wiped them as clean as he could with the piece of rag that served as his handkerchief. He couldn't waste any of his precious water. Champing on one, he entered the mill.

He climbed to the very top to get the best view over the surrounding countryside. This wasn't easy as it meant ascending flimsy ladders encumbered with rifle, backpack, sleeping bag and various pouches. The small window looked out over the fields to a village whose roofs still shone from the rain which had by now stopped. All was still and silent apart from the wind which carried the sounds of distant gunfire. Time to go and find the river again.

Jim collected his gear and took it to the hatch in the floor. He decided to drop his gear, leaving him with just his rifle to carry. But calamity! His backpack hit the ladder and knocked it down. It was too high to jump. Jim was trapped!

The prospect of capture definitely didn't appeal and even if the Germans bypassed the mill, which wasn't likely, getting through their lines, even at night, would be a dangerous undertaking indeed.

Jim looked around, trying not to panic. A box of old papers caught his eye. He investigated and found they seemed to be old bills and invoices, written in Dutch of course. Jim had a brainwave. He fumbled in his pockets until he found a three-inch length of indelible pencil. He sat on the floor and began to make paper aeroplanes out of the larger pieces of paper. After he'd made five, he licked the pencil and wrote on each one: "Help! English soldier trapped in windmill." Then launched them out of the window. A couple fell down among the carrots while the others sailed off on the wind, towards the village Jim hoped. He then repeated this process, five at a time, as fast as he could.

Nearly an hour had passed and Jim was running short of paper. The sporadic gunfire had got a bit louder. He passed another five out and to his great relief saw a man on a horse-drawn cart approaching. At last!

Jim was soon free and thanked Mr Van Oort, the owner of the mill, profusely. Mr Van Oort spoke quite good English and told Jim where the river was, telling him that other villagers were already out, gathering up the paper aeroplanes before the Germans arrived. He then presented Jim with a large loaf of bread and a round of cheese before wishing him luck.

Jim was soon on his way and eventually found his unit. "Where the hell 've you been?" yelled Sergeant Briggs. "I got lost sarge," replied Jim. "Well, don't do it again," came the response as he went off to share his bread and cheese with his mates.

One Too Many

Ron's Discount Shop was very popular within the area of the big town in which he lived and operated. He was always on the lookout for 'gear' and was not fussy from whence it came. At his local pub, Ron was to be seen nearly every evening in the hope of being approached by someone with something to sell. Ron's hero was, somewhat obviously, Arthur Daley from television's 'Minder' series, played superbly by George Cole which he'd recorded on an old VCR recorder, bought cheaply with no questions asked.

Items had to be cheap, of course, so he could sell them cheap and move them on quickly. A typical transaction would go something like: a man or woman would sidle up to Ron at the bar. "A word," he or she would say and take Ron to one side. "Got some gear in the car," and out they'd go to look at it.

After a good look round a car boot would be opened to reveal a television set, tools or any one of a myriad of things which were portable and could be moved on quickly. Once, a good haul of twelve dusty upmarket bottles of port were revealed which, once the seller had gone, Ron turned into a quick profit in the pub. "Put a bottle away for Christmas," he'd say. The publican bought six; Ron sold five of the others to punters and kept one for himself.

Of course, all this was to the detriment and distress of the original owners from whom the 'gear' had been stolen but it wasn't all thus. Ron had a legitimate house clearance business so was able to mix stolen items with legitimate ones to the frustration of the police who by now had a lengthy list of theft reports to deal with. But, in common with most or all rogues, Ron was eventually caught.

He'd had his eye on an abandoned ground floor flat. Not the flat itself which was empty apart from a not-too-old electric cooker.

As there was no 'For Sale or Rent' sign outside and neither did it appear in the local estate agents (Ron checked) he should have smelt a rat, but greed can be a powerful spur to someone like Ron.

One dark moonless night he pulled up outside the flat in his van and quietly unloaded a sack barrow. The credit card trick soon dealt with the Yale lock on the front door of the flat and Ron was in. After ensuring the mains, electricity was turned off he wrenched the cooker cable from the wall, got the cooker on to his sack barrow and soon had it in his van after quietly closing the front door.

He didn't have it, or his liberty, very long. The flat was a police trap and the cooker had been marked by them on its base out of sight. End of the road for Ron's Discount Shop and for Ron too, for four years at least. One hopes that a new leaf was eventually turned over by Ron but do such people ever learn?

Sweet Inspiration

Please Note: the song and the Specials are real.

Gerry often glanced covetously at the jacket displayed in the window of a shop in the town which called itself 'The Macho Shop'. He sometimes did more than just glance too as he imagined himself wearing it. But with a price tag of £385 his dream had to remain just that. To get to work he had a bicycle, anything with an engine in it was beyond his means too, and his job as a trainee welder wasn't exactly overpaid.

Gerry was careful to maintain his bicycle in good order as, apart from his feet, it was his only means of transport. Every Sunday morning he'd clean and oil it, even to the extent of removing the chain, soaking it in a small bowl of petrol, then putting back on and oiling it. The petrol was with permission of his dad who kept it for his lawnmower. Tyres were replaced when worn. Although it was old, having Sturmey-Archer three-speed gears rather than a modern Derailleur, it was Gerry's pride and joy, him having been given it by his grandfather.

One Sunday Gerry had finished his cleaning routine and, following an urgent call of nature, had nipped indoors to use the loo, forgetting to push his bicycle into the front garden. When he came out it had gone!

The rest of Sunday morning and all of the afternoon found Gerry in deep gloom. He searched around and asked his neighbours, but no bicycle. It was a lovely summer's day but that had no effect on him.

After tea, he mooched around the town feeling very low. Then he saw it! Being ridden on by a girl! "Oi!" he shouted, "that's my bike!" The girl turned round and rode over to him. "All right, keep your hair on, I only borrowed it," she said with a grin. "Well you should have asked first," replied the still angry Gerry.

Then he looked more closely at her. Two large blue eyes set in a very pretty face. Gerry's anger subsided and he felt his face begin to burn. "I'm Carol," she said by way of introduction. "Okay, I'm Gerry," he said, taking his bicycle back. "Just ask next time," and rode home.

At home, he kept thinking of her and how graceful she'd looked on his bicycle. He liked music but had never thought of himself as a song writer. But a little jingle with a line of words kept running through his mind. At last, he wrote it down then found, to his surprise, that the rest of the words came easily until he had composed a full-blown song. But what to do with it? Was it any good?

Gerry had a couple of mates who were in a group He'd heard them practicing in the local village hall and thought them pretty good even though they were not on the road yet as their repertoire was not large enough.

Gerry went to see one of them, Ron, and, feeling rather embarrassed, sang the song to him. "That sounds good," said Ron, "come along to our practice tomorrow night."

Gerry did so and the rest of the lads were impressed with his song. They recorded his singing it so's they could learn the words and work out an arrangement. Gerry left them to it and got on with his life although Ron did keep in touch and one day told him the group had an audition with a record company, then later that they had passed it and were going to record his song.

Time passed and one day Gerry was pleasantly surprised when a fat royalty cheque dropped through his letter box followed by others as the song rose up in the charts. He soon had the jacket he coveted and a bit later a used Vespa scooter as well.

He had certainly not forgotten Carol through all this and after he'd passed his test the two of them became a common site around the town on the Vespa.

All this was some years ago. The song was followed by others and now Gerry and Carol being married with two children have replaced the Vespa with a car. The bicycle is still lovingly cared for but not ridden too often these days.

The song? Oh, I nearly forgot. It's *The Push Bike Song* by the 'Specials' the first line of which is: "Riding Along on a Push-Bike, Honey." Well, Carol was a bit special, wasn't she?

A Roman Legacy

Malcolm emerged from the tailors carrying his new pin-stripe suit. Old fashioned and not quite the thing for his forthcoming wedding but a new suit was a must and he'd got it cheap as it was a cancelled order which luckily was his size.

Money – or rather the lack of it – was an ongoing problem for Malcolm. His job as a filing clerk with a finance company wasn't well paid and it offered little chance of promotion. This did not deter him from getting married and his fiancée, Dorothy, was of the same mind.

Dorothy could only walk short distances with great difficulty due to a childhood riding accident. She spent most of her time in a wheelchair either reading history books or knitting. She did what chores as she was able and was a competent cook. Outside, Malcolm pushed her wheelchair. There was nothing wrong with her mind or her determination to marry Malcolm. "We'll get along somehow," she'd say when Malcolm expressed doubts for the future. "Love conquers all and ours is as strong as anyone else's."

Accommodation wasn't a problem, except for its upkeep, as Malcolm had inherited a very small two-bed roomed bungalow from his parents. The garden was mostly laid out to lawn as they had had no interest in gardening. Dorothy had moved in with him some three months before and on this day was cooking a meal of tripe and onions for them both, a cheap meal which they both happened to like.

Malcolm made his way home on the bus. Taxis, in common with car ownership, were out of the question. He wore his old straw boater and was glad of it on this hot day. Others may laugh at it but Malcolm didn't care, it did its job.

Back home, the betrothed pair ate their meal with home home-made apple pie to follow, then Malcolm said: "I think I'll have a dip in the sea then get on with the garden."

"Okay," replied Dorothy with a twinkle in her eye, "that gets you out of the washing up!"

Malcolm had determined to grow vegetables to eke out their finances. He'd bought some old tools from a car boot sale plus a book by Alan Titchmarsh and, refreshing swim over, he got down to it.

The ground was quite soft under the turf which Malcolm had removed the evening before. His first dig and his spade hit something hard. He scraped the earth away to reveal a regular series of small, red, oblong stones. Enlarging the hole revealed more of them. *Oh hell,* he thought, *these are going to be a nuisance.*

He went and fetched Dorothy who hobbled out on her crutches. "They look Roman," she said excitedly on peering into the hole, "we need to report them."

A phone call to the local museum soon brought a lady from there to look and who quickly reported Malcolm's find to the County Archaeologist. A proper excavation was organised which revealed a lovely Roman mosaic floor of red baked clay tiles with an intricate pattern in black ones. "There must have been a very small villa here," said the excavation director. "I'm sorry but you won't be able to grow anything here, it's too shallow."

But this was not really bad news. English Heritage paid Malcolm a handsome compensation plus a yearly stipend to leave the mosaic untouched which was accurately drawn to scale and photographed before the earth and turf was replaced. The money paid for a purpose-built kitchen for Dorothy and the couple's finances were eased. Malcolm still wore his straw boater, but not to the wedding of course. His pin-striped suit sufficed for that. Well, no point in wasting money, is there?

Did God Invent the Bicycle

Of all the contraptions invented by man the bicycle must be near the top of the ludicrous list – if indeed there is one.

It's not the machine itself but rather the ridiculous posture its rider is forced to adopt. The back is bent like that of a deformed dwarf while the head is ricked up as if it's just received a stiff uppercut. The posterior sticks out in a most unnatural fashion while the knees pump up and down in the manner of demented pistons. Unflattering skin-tight shorts and a silly hat complete the ensemble.

The view from the rear is no less humorous, especially if the rider is forced to stand up whilst pedalling. Then the backside sways left and right as do two balloons on a pendulum and if the rider is very overweight then the phrase 'two little boys fighting under a blanket' comes to mind (excuse me while I have hysterics!).

But does God have a sense of humour? A couple of examples should show that he has.

The nose. This gristly protuberance, which precedes us every time we move forwards, seems to have two main functions.

First is a sense of smell which we are told is important. But when I think of the obnoxious odours which emanated from the nether regions of the coarser of my schoolfellows, and much later from their adult counterparts and all accompanied by loud guffaws of laughter; I often wished I didn't have one – a sense of smell that is.

Its second function is to run. It does this whenever its owner catches a cold, suffers from hay fever or a dust etc. allergy. It then produces copious amounts of an evil gunge called mucus, forces its owner to emit all sorts of awful snorting and honking noises that have no place in polite society and advertises the fact by glowing bright red! Couldn't God have located it somewhere more discreet, in an armpit, for instance? No, He has to plant it right in the middle of the face!

The nose does have secondary functions, one of which is to provide a support for spectacles. Without it those of us who abhor contact lenses would have to wear goggles, which do not enhance anybody's appearance.

Then there's the ears. Useful for being flicked and tweaked by said coarse schoolfellows, not to mention one or two irate teachers, but little else. We can't even flap them to keep cool in the manner of elephants. So they remain as something else for us to laugh at although I do suppose they prevent one's hat falling over one's eyes.

But we do have a solution – hair. We can grow it long enough to cover the offending flaps although that doesn't help Yul Brynner types. Perhaps they could grow a piece each side. This would leave us with a rather odd-looking man. Bald, except for a hank of hair each side, his nose under his arm and wearing goggles! No, I think we'll leave things as they are.

I think the foregoing does show that God does have a sense of humour which reinforces my view that he did indeed invent the bicycle.

A Very Memorable Day

I didn't get to go abroad until quite late, the end of the 1990s, I think it was. Some friends of ours suggested we make a foursome and go on a guided tour of some of the cemeteries, museums and sites relating to the First World War. Having had an interest in this and other wars since my schooldays I jumped at it and my wife was enthusiastic too. And so it was arranged.

The day of departure found us bowling along the roads of southern England in excited anticipation of our adventure. Then a change of coach, through the channel tunnel, then France into Belgium where we spent our first night.

We found our room then went out to explore, taking in the signs we couldn't read, cars driving on the wrong side of the road, a cobbled public square with fountains which periodically squirted into the air from holes in the ground and tables and chairs belonging to adjacent cafes full of people eating, drinking and, most of all, chattering.

The next day was the start of our tour, a great contrast to our first day. We first visited a large military cemetery, a sad and sombre place, yet with a beauty all of its own with immaculate lawns, thousands of white gravestones all standing in serried ranks like soldiers on parade. Each one had a small rose growing in front of it; its shadow moving across the stone as the sun moved across the sky.

This cemetery is known as Tyne Cott because the now sealed German pillbox at its centre was dubbed Tyne Cottage by our lads during the war. Many other places were also given British names at the time.

The young ages of many of the dead was shocking. In places two, three, four or more stones were placed next to each other. This was where it had proved impossible to separately identify the remains – no DNA in those days – just their identity discs proved whom they had been. God knows in what horrible circumstances they had died. The War to End All Wars? If only! There was still another World War to come and plenty of others before and since. Maybe the human race hates itself. Frank Sinatra once said that bigotry is the biggest enemy of the human race but I think bigotry stems from intolerance, which is the real enemy.

We then moved on to the place where many of the guys in the cemetery had died, just another anonymous field which had been ploughed and harrowed. It was on a slope and another sealed German pillbox at the top showed that they had had the advantage of the high ground.

Our guide described what had happened here and pointed out where the trenches had been. Many soldiers from both sides still lay there, their remains never had been found. I wandered away from the group and walked quite a way into the field. It was a very hot, still day and, apart from a faint hum of voices from the group, silent. Then I realised there were no birds, perhaps they avoided the place, their instinct telling them it was a place to be avoided. In the far distance some buildings – a village? – shimmered in the heat haze, rather like streamers dancing in the wind of a fan. It was like walking on holy ground. *This is where they all died,* I said to myself as a wave of sadness washed over me. In the peaceful stillness, it was hard to imagine the raging horror that once roared over this land.

I noticed thousands of lead balls on the ground – lead shrapnel. Shrapnel shells exploded in the air, sending their lethal charge shooting forward, redolent of a giant shotgun. Here was a small brass buckle from a haversack, green with age, there a rusty ring with a large pin attached from the tailgate of a lorry or, more probably, a horse-drawn cart.

A swishing noise from the bottom of the slope caught my ear then my eye. A small clump of trees with moving foliage although I felt no wind. I shivered and at that moment a shout from the coach told me it was time to go.

I gave a last though to the poor souls still laying there. Did their shades emerge at night to re-fight their invisible, silent battles? I left the field and walked along its edge. There I saw a Mills hand grenade, complete but very rusty and still very lethal. At the corner, a small heap of also very rusty and very lethal unexploded shells also awaited collection by the authorities. This was part of the iron harvest which will be deactivated or blown up. They already have a 15-year backlog.

The rest of the week showed us other such sites, cemeteries plus museums and over the succeeding years the four of us made several similar trips, to World War II sites etc. on those times. All were interesting, sad and sombre but I never forgot that first day, the day I walked with ghosts.

Waste Not Want Not

Bernie was what people variously called a fossiker, a fertler, a scrounger or 'Old Dumpy'. He didn't care a hoot what people called him as he pushed his old barrow here and there wearing an old deerstalker hat he'd found on a local dump. It made him feel like a sort of Sherlock Holmes, seeking saleables rather than criminals.

Bernie eked out a precarious living by just hunting around virtually everywhere where he thought he might find anything he could sell.

Wherever there was a dump or a household recycling unit Bernie would be found rooting around. Even fly-tipping sites sometimes produced an oddment or two that could be turned into cash.

He certainly wasn't welcome everywhere. Council employees would sometimes chase him away from the recycling unit. "If you get hurt," the foreman once said to him in a very stern voice, "there'll be hell to pay because you're not covered by our insurance." It was no good Bernie protesting that he'd be careful and "wasn't doin' no 'arm," the foreman wasn't prepared to take on the responsibility.

But the foreman wasn't always there. The unit was open seven days each week and the foreman worked only five. The other guys turned a blind eye. "Is bleedin' fault if 'e gets 'urt," one of them said, "I didn't see 'im, did I?"

Bernie became something of an expert on all sorts of things, both old and new. Brass, copper and lead went to the local scrap merchant and even antiques were not beyond his remit. Part of a tea set by Charlotte Rhead fetched £15 at a local auction. People who broke one of a pair of vases often threw its companion away even though singles sometimes had a value as Bernie well knew.

Bernie sometime sold items directly to the public himself. A large shed in his garden contained all sorts of things he'd found over the years, some of which were hard to sell, others not. A stainless steel sink top fetched £8 and Bernie got £10 for a little wall cupboard he'd found which only needed a quick coat of cheap white paint. He'd even got the paint free, a half-empty tin thrown on a dump. A sign on his gate said, "Used Items For Sale" which attracted more browsers than buyers but there were enough of the latter to make it just about worthwhile. Bernie took the sign down when he went 'A-huntin'' as he called it.

Bernie had an old metal detector he called 'Tecky' which he'd not used for ages. He'd never found anything worthwhile and the jar of old pennies and ha'pennies he'd found over the years remained unsold. Old silver coins could be sold for scrap but Bernie had never found enough to make the ten mile trip to his nearest coin dealer worthwhile. He found his 'a-huntin'' of old dumps much more effective.

At the local river, which was very shallow, Bernie waded in and searched downstream from the bridge as he knew people sometimes threw coins in for luck, a habit which dates from Celtic times where they believed a god lived in the river. He found a few old pennies. "Huh," he said to himself, "they wouldn't get much luck with that." He did find a nice silver shilling bearing the stern profile of Queen Victoria on one side and the date 1898 on the other. Bernie decided to keep that for good luck.

He also found a brass wedding ring and wondered how it had got there. People in times past who couldn't afford gold used these, changing them for gold ones if and when they became better off.

Bernie gave up on 'Tecky' and searched around eyes only. Lots of junk, how untidy people were! What looked like an upturned wok turned out to be an old satellite dish. Plenty of bottles but no old ones which Bernie knew could be turned into cash. He did find one though, to his great delight. This was an old ink bottle – empty of course – and fashioned in the shape of a little house with doors and windows all fashioned in the glass. The chimney was where a pen or quill would have been dipped in. "Wow!" said Bernie aloud, "a cottage ink in perfect nick. Twenty quid of anyone's money." He knew just the dealer to take it to.

Bernie decided to call it a day, he was very hot and his local with its cold lager wasn't far away. He clambered up the bank, giving an old feather mattress that lay there a desultory kick. "Scruffy gits," he said to himself.

To his surprise a slit opened up. Bernie looked closer. It had obviously been cut and stitched up again; the water must have rotted the stitches. Something inside! Bernie pulled it out, a packet in some waterproof material tied tightly with string. Bernie used his penknife to cut the string and, to his great surprise, a thick wad of very old white five pound notes was revealed!

Being honest, Bernie took them to the police. They were never claimed despite local media publicity so Bernie got them back.

At a specialist coin and banknote auction the notes, sold individually, fetched £62,000 after commission. Bernie sold his cottage and bought a shop with accommodation in the nearest large town, setting himself up as a pukka antiques dealer. With his knowledge, success was assured and he became a very rich man.

He died of a heart attack aged 88.

They found him with a Victorian shilling clutched in his hand.

Mrs Ferguson's Tea Set

Prior to their entry to World War II, the Japanese, being anxious to extend their empire, were undecided as to whether they should expand south-east and attack the United States at Pearl Harbour and the Philippines or go north and attack Russia. Opinion was divided but when the Germans attacked Russia in June 1941 it seemed to present a favourable opportunity for Japan to do likewise.

But there were those who thought the Germans couldn't win and felt that the USA was the easier option. They did form the majority view but with reservations. Enter Mrs Ferguson's tea set.

Mr & Mrs Ferguson were passengers on an armed merchant cruiser called the SS 'Mara' which was carrying a very varied cargo, including munitions, when she was challenged by the German surface raider 'Atlantis'.

The 'Mara' made the mistake of firing her single 4-inch gun at the 'Atlantis' which immediately replied with a salvo from her 5.9 inch guns, disabling the 'Mara' and killing some of her crew. She was then boarded by men from the 'Atlantis' who took items they wanted, such as frozen meat, and took the passengers and remaining crew aboard their own vessel.

As they were unable to salvage the 'Mara' the Germans prepared to scuttle her but Mrs Ferguson went to their captain and begged him to save their luggage which contained a valuable and cherished tea set. The captain agreed and ordered his men to follow Mrs Ferguson's instructions as to the location of the luggage room, brushing aside the protestations of a British officer who knew what else was in the room.

The room was found, its door blown off and the Ferguson's two suitcases recovered. But so was something else, mail bags, some of which had been officially sealed.

One large obstacle holding back the Japanese was British forces stationed in the east that might well attack their flank if they attacked the US. The Germans ashore studied the official documents recovered from the 'Mara' and found they contained complete and detailed dispositions of the British Eastern Forces.

They passed these to the Japanese who were delighted to see that our forces were far weaker than they had supposed. There was even a statement saying we would not be able to hold Singapore in the event of Japanese attack. Greatly relieved, the Japanese attacked Pearl Harbour.

The Fergusons and their precious tea set survived the war.

Grand Daddy's Tooth

Please note the spelling and grammatical errors are deliberate

Back in the 20s us kids would go to Granddaddy's in the summer.

Mom and pop would drop us off'n the buggy and it would be just us kids and Granddaddy for five or six weeks 'cos Grandma was dead and Granddaddy buried her in the woods with his own two hands.

Granddaddy's house was actually a big shack which had been built by his granddaddy so was pretty old. We all slept in hammocks which was great while Granddaddy had his big double bed. The shack was up in the backwoods of Kentucky and was nowhere anywheres or near anywheres else. We kids loved it there, no neatening up for school or church and no having to be anywheres at any particular time.

There was four of us. Tom was the oldest then Billy then Lucy which is me then Joe Boy. We played in the woods, clumb the trees and lived pretty wild. We stayed together which kept us safe and I never got left out just 'cause I was a girl.

We learned the names of all the plants and always put some wild flowers on Grandma's grave while praying to Jesus to look after her immortal soul. I was but two when she went so I never knew her much at all. We could also name the birds and animals and who which to stay clear of and tell them by their footprints. Granddaddy called them 'spoor' but footprints was fine by me.

Things got even better when our cousins come. There were three of them and were Dennis, Alice who was about the same age as me and little Eddie. Dennis seemed to like me and would betimes give me a smile and a wink which would make me feel happy and wish I had on my pretty blue church dress instead of my old dungarees.

Sometimes, Granddaddy would lend the older boys his old Winchester rifle which was a hand me down from his daddy and we'd go off looking for jackrabbits. The rifle was only single shot .22 calibre so you had to be right on first shot else the bunny would be gone afore you could reload. The boys would usually get three of four on ’em and we’d take ’em back to Granddaddy who’d skin and gut ’em then cut ’em up and toss ’em in a big pot with some of his home grown vegetables and herbs and water then put the pot on his old black stove to simmer away for a good while.

When it started to get dark, the boys would get a goodly camp fire going ‘n when it burnt down to a hot embers bed Granddaddy would take the pot to the fire by a bit of wood through the handle and dump it on the embers to ‘finish off’ as he used to say. We’d all set around on logs trying to fergit our hunger and by and by Granddaddy would dump a good portion out of the pot on to each of our tin plates and we ate it with hunks of his home baked corn bread for dipping in. They was the best dinners I ever ate.

Afterwards we’d all set around and listen to Granddaddy’s stories of the old days. Sometimes he’d keep his pipe in and it would bob up and down like nothun’ you’ve ever seen. He’d talk about his time in the big war too and at those times Dennis would look at me and pull a face which meant Granddaddy was talking stretchers. I didn’t care about that them was good stories, stretchers or not. I found out later that Granddaddy would’ve been too old fer the war but I was only seven and didn’t know how old men had to be to fight ’specially as I once see old Baldy Etherington whup the daylights out of Tommy Burns for a sassing of him. Tommy was big and strong and was sure surprised!

One day we all played baseball and that included Granddaddy who was pretty spry for his age which must have been the wrong side of seventy although I never asked him ’cause that would’ve been rude. It was quite something to see him hopping about in the weedy patch when the ball went his way but after a spell he suddenly yelled, “Oh no!”

We stopped went over and he said “I lost my tooth,” then pulled his mouth back to show us the gap. “Ya won’t be a – growing of a new one,” said Billy and Granddaddy said: “Ya dumb cluck it’s a gold one. Ya Grandma had it made for me a score ’n more years ago.” He bent and poked about in the weeds. We all got down on our knees and did likewise until we covered that that weedy patch but no tooth. “Maybe you trod on it Granddaddy and pushed it under,” said Alice which was a good thought so the boys went to the lean-to for tools and came back with small hand forks and trowels for us young ’uns and they had them spades with long handles which didn’t end with a T or a D.

Well, we dug that patch over good. Granddaddy walked up and down saying, "She'll a-haunt me if it ain't found and I ain't ever gonna get no rest. She used to make me show it to her every week so she knowed I ain't pawned it fer beer."

We sifted the dirt through our fingers but found no durned tooth (excuse my language but it was a very hot day). We had to give up and Granddaddy looked so sad I wanted to cry and I could see Alice did too. He sort of slumped and stuck his hands in his pockets. Then his face lit up and he pulled his left hand out and said, "Well I'll be Dad blamed I musta put it there for safe and fergit I done it." We looked it was gold all right with a little clip to hold it in place. "Wow!" said Granddaddy, "I really got my tooth!" I caught Dennis' eye he had a knowing look on his face. He said: "Yeah Grandpaw ya got ya tooth back an' you also got your ole weedy patch dugged over."

Granddaddy went all red and laughed his wheezy laugh. I see how he had fooled us and we all went in to wash up feeling pretty stupid.

Granddaddy died a couple of years ago and mom and pop buried him next to Grandma. His gold tooth got buried with him. There was a parson too. We still go up there sometimes and put flowers on but we don't stay long as the shack's overgrown and kinda spooky. I still love Granddaddy and I know Alice does too.

Thank you for reading my story and good bye.

Lucy Armitage aged 12 Brownsville, Kentucky 1932.

Alone

Eleanor inserted the key in the latch, turned it to open the door and entered the house.

"I'm ho—" she called then stopped. There was no one there, the house was empty; they had buried Billy the day before.

Quiet.

Still.

Silent.

With a heavy heart, Eleanor sat down at the table, placing her bag on the floor. She looked at Billy's chair and in her mind's eye saw him sitting there in his relaxed way, or having a nap after dinner.

Tears.

Alone.

Lonely.

What bleak words they were!

Thirteen years they'd been together, Eleanor and Billy. Now he'd gone and an empty life stretched ahead.

Solitude.

No one to talk to.

Another partner? No, no one could replace Billy and it would be like she was relegating him to the past – a phase. Move on? No, it would be like she was leaving Billy behind and she couldn't do that.

Alone.

That awful word again.

But would Billy want her to be isolated, lonely, sad?

No, he wouldn't.

That decided the matter.

She would get another partner even though she'd never forget Billy.

His photograph would still remain in pride of place on the mantelpiece so everyone could see how handsome he had been.

Her heart lifted slightly, the decision was definitely made.

She got up, went to the sideboard, got out the Yellow Pages and looked up 'Kittens for Sale'.

A Lonely Lady

Jessica lived alone. It wasn't really through choice but she and George had agreed on an amicable split six months previously. She had, somewhat reluctantly, given him his ring back and sometimes still looked ruefully at the empty third finger of her left hand.

Her cottage was on the outskirts of the village, a bit lonely but that suited Jessica who preferred the noises of the countryside to those of people.

Only two things intruded into her otherwise peaceful life, a morbid fear of spiders and a man who walked past her cottage twice each weekday but made no attempt to speak to her and to Jessica's somewhat fervid imagination seemed to have a sinister aura emanating from him as she peeped from behind her curtains as he passed.

Jessica had another ring. A diamond solitaire which she wore on her right hand. She always took it off at night and sometimes in the daytime too, always leaving it on a little table next to her bed in her downstairs bedroom. It was a family heirloom.

One morning she set off to the village to do her shopping, passing the 'sinister' man on the way. He said nothing as they passed, giving her a grimace which sent a chill up and down her spine.

On her way back home, carrying two large bags of shopping, she remembered her ring and assumed she'd forgotten to put it on.

Reaching home she put her bags down and went to get the ring. It had gone! Frantically she searched the floor, drawers and virtually everywhere to no avail. Horror! It must have been stolen! The sinister man! He'd seen her going to the village carrying her bags and nobody locked their doors in this quiet place. She pondered on what to do next, feeling very lonely indeed. The police? The talk of the village? She imagined what they'd say, "Stupid woman, fancy leaving that lying about."

Thinking about it she packed her shopping away then went to empty the bin in the dustbin. As she approached it a sudden gleam caught her eye. It came from a gap between the edge of the path and the wall. She looked closer. It was the ring! It must have slipped off her finger earlier, perhaps caught on one of the shopping bag handles. She reached down for the ring but as she did so something moved. A big black spider! She jumped back and screamed aloud which brought someone running. The sinister man!

"What's the matter miss?" he said. She pointed and said in a tremulous voice: "Spider!"

He bent down, brushed the spider away and retrieved the ring saying, "Is this what you're looking for?" She took it gratefully and noted that close up he didn't look sinister at all.

She thanked him and invited him in for a cup of tea. He told her his name was Jim (short for James) and she felt herself warming to him. To judge from the twinkle in his eye it was quite possible that the empty space on her left hand would, in due course, be filled!

Never judge by appearances.

A Lone American

George liked his home and didn't want to leave it although he had considered it in the light of the large volume of traffic that thundered past almost continuously. George was from Texas and had decided to remain in England after his time in the American Air Force had expired. He liked the east of England, the quiet countryside and sleepy villages, an ideal place for a peaceful retirement.

Or rather it had been peaceful until it was decided to turn the main road into a dual-carriageway – a big job – and in the meantime traffic would be diverted along the lane past George's house. The large lorries were the worst and sometimes George would go outside and wave his stick angrily at them. The drivers would just laugh or wave back in a pseudo-friendly manner.

One day, quite early in the morning, there was an awful grinding noise from an Eddie Stobart lorry which George plainly heard as he was in his garden. The lorry had stopped outside his cottage.

The driver jumped down from his cab and called to George: "'Scuse me mate, can I use your phone? No mobile signal here, gearbox is shot." George felt like telling him to go away but good old American hospitality prevailed and he invited the driver in.

The driver telephoned then told George the lorry was not repairable at the roadside and the breakdown truck would be two hours getting there. George wasn't dismayed, a bit of company made a nice change. "Have you breakfasted?" he inquired. "Nope," came the reply, "that was going to be my next stop." George immediately went to the kitchen and busied himself with eggs, bacon and hash browns and put a lump of his sourdough into the oven to bake. George had learned to make sourdough bread as a child back home in Texas and had kept up the habit ever since.

The two men ate their breakfast then settled down with coffee for a chat. The driver noted George's accent and told him he had American relations too. George told him that he had joined the air force when his parents had died and over the years had gradually lost contact with his sister back in Texas.

The driver asked to use the loo and went upstairs to do so. His eye caught a large faded photograph in an old brown frame on the wall outside. He started, stooped and looked closer, his eyes widening in surprise.

After using the loo, he rushed downstairs and said to George: “That old photo up there, would it be of you and your sister?”

“Yes,” replied George, surprised at the driver’s excitement.

“That were me and Dolores back home jest after ma ’n pa had gone. Why?”

“I think she may be my gran,” said the driver, “she’s called Dolores too!”

George was dumbfounded. Dolores? After all these years? The tear-evoking memories came flooding back. The clapboard house, the Texas sun and the stews with sourdough bread.

There isn’t much more to tell. One happy day an elderly lady who, like George, was very tall came walking up to his open door together with her husband, also ex-American Air Force stationed in Britain. Then a joyful reunion, tears and an afternoon filled with memories and catching up. The driver, Bill, and George became firm friends and Bill knew where he could always get a free breakfast.

Small world, isn’t it?

A First Contact

Sergeant Kowalski glared at the soldier standing to attention in front of his desk, removed the long-dead cigar stub from his mouth, dropped it into the waste bin and growled: "What d'yer want, Simmonds?"

Private First Class Ronald Simmonds said: "We think we got a hit. You need to tell the colonel."

"You only think? You do know it's the colonel's nap time?"

"Then you can say we definitely have a hit, sir."

"The hell you have!" (Kowalski was a big fan of John Wayne). He heaved his bulk out of his chair, to which he normally seemed welded, took four steps to a door marked 'Colonel Roberts', knocked and went in.

A few moments later he emerged followed by a middle-aged man with steel grey hair that matched his eyes. He said: "What's your name soldier and what've you got?"

"PFC Simmonds, sir. Three beeps at one second intervals. After three seconds, we get three back, same frequency, lower pitch."

"Three seconds you say?" Said the colonel, "that's pretty damn close. You sure you ain't got a bouncer?"

"No sir," replied Simmonds, "there's nothing in that part of space."

"Right, follow me," said the colonel, "you too Kowalski."

The three of them left the office and walked down a short corridor which brought them to a door which the colonel opened using his security card. The few technicians inside sprang to attention as he entered followed by Kowalski and Simmonds. "Relax," he said.

The room was the centre of a highly secret base in the Nevada desert where, under the acronym SETI (the Search for Extra Terrestrial Intelligence) the Americans searched for alien life while publicly denying they were doing so.

"Well?" said the colonel to a female radio operator.

"Briggs, sir," she replied as she flipped a switch. Through a speaker came three echoing beeps, rather like underwater sonar. After a short delay, three low beeps came back.

"The hell it is!" said the colonel, who was also a big fan of John Wayne, "Gimmee a cigar Kowalski," and turning to a technician said: "Lockdown."

The technician flipped a switch which sealed the two entrances to the base and cut off the land lines. The colonel didn't want some rookie to earn himself a few bucks by blabbing to the press. Cell phones etc. were banned.

Kowalski handed a cigar over which the colonel stuck in his mouth without lighting it. He always looked after the colonel's cigars and was thus able to snaffle the odd one for himself.

"Voicecom," ordered the colonel. Jane Briggs sat down, switched on her microphone and said: "Hello, this is the planet we call Earth. We are receiving your signal, can you understand me?"

A nasal, tinny voice replied: "Hello Earth, yes, we understand you. We note you have not mastered interstellar travel so we visit you. We are very close and do not have much time because we note your planet is surrounded by a strong magnetic field which means we will not be able to communicate with you once we enter it. Landing coordinates please."

"Wait please," said Briggs, looking at the colonel.

"Give 'em the gravel," he said.

The gravel was a large square of that material outside the colonel's office. He'd had the grass removed because the lawn mowers interrupted his afternoon naps.

Briggs rose and crossed to the huge plan of the base on the wall. Noting the precise co-ordinates on her pad she returned to her seat and read them into her microphone.

"Thank you," said the tinny voice. "Our vessel is a bright silver sphere or ball designed to deflect the solar wind and reflect radiation. We will be with you in one hour and twenty-one minutes precisely."

"Dress uniforms," ordered the colonel and in one hour the three men were standing by the gravel, all showered and looking very smart.

The minutes ticked by, seemingly very slowly, but at last the great moment arrived. And – nothing!

"The Goddamn thing's invisible!" exclaimed the colonel. Kowalski went to move forward but the colonel stopped him saying: "Hold hard, Kowalski, I'll handle this." And with that he walked slowly from one corner to another with hands outstretched. Nothing, so he repeated the process with the other two corners. Then he walked up and down, getting more exasperated by the minute.

Finally, he stood in the centre of the gravel and yelled: "A hoax! A Goddamn hoax! Kowalski, I want every man and woman on this base interrogated until their teeth fall out! Ya got me?"

"Yes, sir," said Kowalski, his dreams of a cushy posting vanishing like smoke on a windy day.

The colonel stomped off, his heavy boots crunching on the gravel. But one thing his boot crunched wasn't a piece of gravel.

It was a tiny silver ball.

A Bird in the Hand

Jimmy's bird was an extremely rare one although he didn't know it. He had found it in his garden one day being attacked by a group of sparrows. The bird was bright green and red which was surely the reason it had been attacked. He shooed the sparrows away which left only the coloured bird which had been slightly injured in one wing. He got a shoe box from the house, punched some holes in it then used it to trap the bird. He already had a budgerigar so he put some of its seeds and a saucer of water in the box and was glad to see the bird go for both.

Bit by bit, the bird recovered so Jimmy bought it its own cage in case the budgie took exception to it and the bird seemed perfectly happy there, chirping and chattering away to itself.

Now Jimmy had a friend, Ben, who was very much a bird fancier. He and Jimmy worked together and sometimes socialised out of work.

Jimmy told Ben about the bird and Ben hastened round to see it. He immediately recognised it for what it was but said nothing to Jimmy as he knew it was worth a great deal of money to the right people. He determined to steal the bird!

Ben took the next morning off. He knew the layout of Jimmy's house and using his credit card opened the Yale lock and gained entry. In his pocket, he had a sock to carry the bird in which would prevent it flapping its wings and hopefully keep it quiet until he could get away.

When Jimmy came home for lunch, he was horrified to see the empty cage and searched high and low in the house and garden but to no avail. He couldn't find any way the bird could have got out but couldn't bring himself to suspect Ben, his best friend. Sadly, he resigned himself to his loss.

Meanwhile, Ben was driving out of the city to a pre-arranged rendezvous with a dealer who was prepared to give him £5,000 for the bird subject to examining it. Then: Traffic!

It was always like this at this time of the afternoon. The bird was quiescent in the sock which Ben had secured by tying the neck with string.

It was a very hot day and, despite the car's fan, it soon got stifling inside so Ben opened his window. He nearly jumped out of his skin when a flash of green and red hurtled past his face and out of the open window. In his haste to lay hands on the bird, he had grabbed the first sock in his drawer he had come to, failing to notice a small hole in the toe. The bird, possibly the possessor of a greater degree of intelligence than Ben, had simply enlarged the hole, got out, and awaited its chance.

Back home, Jimmy was sitting looking mournfully at the empty cage; he hadn't had the heart to go back to work.

Suddenly, there was a tapping at the window. Jimmy looked up. The bird! He let it in whereupon it flew into its cage, drank some water and resumed its happy chirping and chattering.

In the meantime, Jimmy had been thinking. He thought it odd that Ben hadn't been at work that morning. He resolved to buy chains for his doors.

Meanwhile Ben had determined to learn to darn socks!

Pie in the Sky

Barney was fascinated by the moon, in fact one could say obsessed. It had all started when, as a small child, he was given a half-decent telescope complete with tripod and instruction book one Christmas.

Having reached the limitations of his basic telescope, he soon got tired of the stars and Jupiter with its red spot and four Galilean moons because nothing changed much. The moon was a different matter, so much to see! Craters, mountain ranges and huge plains the ancients called 'mares' because they thought they were seas.

People teased him. One uncle told him the moon was made of green cheese but Barney didn't fall for that. He knew cheese was made from milk and milk came from cows. He was sure there were no cows on the moon!

He went through a stage of wanting to go to the moon but the story of The Boy who wanted the Moon changed all that. It goes like this:

"There was once a little boy who had very rich parents who doted on him. They gave him everything he wanted, toys, sweets, cakes, whatever all the year round and not just at Christmas and birthdays. But one early evening in winter he saw the full moon and wanted that. He cried when he couldn't get it as he had no conception of not being able to have anything he wanted. He refused to eat so his very worried parents tricked him with a balloon with a light inside which they placed on top of his wardrobe, ensuring the curtains were closed tight on moonlit nights."

"But one fateful night the maid failed to close the curtains properly and when the boy saw a sliver of light shining through he got out of bed to investigate and there, up in the sky, was the moon!"

"He immediately began to wail and wouldn't stop and there was nothing his parents could do about it, no amount of new toys or sweets had any effect. His mouth got bigger and bigger until he seemed to be all mouth and, refusing to eat, he died."

Barney thought both the boy and his parents were stupid. He should have realised he couldn't have everything and they shouldn't have spoiled him.

Jules Verne's *The First Men in the Moon* really fired Barney's imagination. A race of people called Selenites who lived underground. Maybe they lived on boats on a vast lake. Perhaps some of the craters were ruins from the day when people were able to live on the surface, assuming the moon once had an atmosphere.

He learned where Selene came from. The ancient Greeks believed that the twin gods, Artemis and Apollo, were supposed to take turns driving the chariot of Sol, the sun, across the sky so that it shone all the time. But Artemis – who the Romans called Diana – wasn't interested as all she wanted to do was hunt so she had the lesser god, Selene to stand in for her but, unlike the twins, Selene didn't shed light and could only shine by reflected light, a pale imitation of Sol, and even that wasn't always available.

Barney was enthralled by all these stories and spent many night-time hours with only his telescope and imagination for company. Then, great excitement! The Americans were going to send men to the moon and in July 1969 they did.

On the night of the launch, Barney stayed up all through it, his mind ablaze with euphoria. What would they find? Some sort of Selenites? What might they bring back? Some sort of being might have problems with our atmospheric pressure and our gravity is six times that of the moon. What would they look like? Would Barney get to meet him or her? All sorts of things crossed his mind.

Then the astronauts returned and what did they bring? Rocks and dust! Barney's world collapsed. Is that all? He could go to the beach if he wanted to see rocks and there was plenty of dust in the Hoover bag. What a let-down! Suddenly the moon lost all its attraction. Barney gave all his astronomy books to a local charity shop and relegated his telescope to the spare room. As it had been a present he couldn't dispose of it.

So dear reader, dreams are fine because they sometimes come true and imaginations can, on occasion, become reality. Just don't rely on them!

A Timely Tale

Robin and Duncan were two gay men who lived happily together and had done so for some years. They had met through cricket, both playing for their local team.

Cooking, washing, cleaning and gardening were all chores that were shared and away from their respective jobs both men had skills which they practiced to good effect. Robin was a landscape painter while Duncan repaired old clocks he'd bought at boot fairs then set them into wooden surrounds which he carved into leaves, berries, birds and small animals. The pair would take their products to the local Saturday market from time to time where they were eagerly snapped up by the locals.

One thing the two men vehemently disagreed on was music. Robin was a classical aficionado and refused to have any other kind in the house. He specially hated rock 'n roll, saying: "That was where all this modern rubbish started. To think this abomination uses the same eight notes as Mozart did." In vain did Duncan protest.

"But there was music before that, lots of it," he would say. "Jazz, country, folk."

"All low-brow stuff," Robin would retort (he was a bit of a snob); "you should lift your mind."

But Duncan didn't want to lift his mind so he played his radio whilst working in the shed he used as a workshop and never went with Robin to concerts.

One day Duncan went for a walk to stretch his legs. Robin was off painting somewhere. He walked up the mountain as the locals called it, in reality a hill, marvelling at the coloured striations that showed in some of the scattered stones. Then an idea came to him. Grinning to himself he looked closer and at last found what he wanted, an irregularly-shaped flat stone with some nice striations.

He carried it home and selected a clock from his small stock, an old-fashioned wind-up type with at its back a winder, a knob to alter the time and a lever to render it fast or slow.

He set to work on the stone with masonry drills and Dremel tool until he had made a hole through it into which the clock just fitted. He polished the stone and flattened its base so it would stand up. He then varnished it and glued the clock in place resulting in a clock that was very attractive although somewhat heavy.

Upon seeing it, Robin was enthralled. "Wow, that's brilliant!" he exclaimed, "Please don't sell it." He took it and stood it on the mantelpiece, relegating the old clock to the next market day. Duncan grinned inwardly.

One very hot evening a barbecue was proposed and enacted, Robin doing the cooking while Duncan prepared the salad and two bottles of wine and ice from the fridge in an ice box he had constructed.

When everything was nearly ready, the noise of the gate latch made the pair look up. It was Briony, Duncan's sister, who sometimes called for tea and a chat. Upon being asked to partake of the barbecue, she enthusiastically acquiesced and a convivial evening was had by all.

By and by, the food and wine were used and the ice melted so the trio retired indoors for coffee.

Briony gasped when she spied the clock. "Oh I do like that!" she exclaimed.

"Yes," said Robin, "Duncan made it, isn't he clever?"

"Lovely piece of stone," said Briony, touching it. "Rock Around the Clock."

The atmosphere suddenly went cold. Robin caught Duncan blushing with a sheepish grin on his face. "So that's it!" he exclaimed angrily and made to pick the clock up.

Briony stopped him. "No, don't," she pleaded, "it's still a great work of art." So Robin, with bad grace, set it down again. He never did see the funny side and it took him two days to get over it. The clock stayed on the mantelpiece but the music remained relegated to the shed!

Brown's Folly

Alf Brown was very proud of his new uniform and to be part, albeit a very small one, of the organisation that had won the Battle of Britain even though in the latter half of 1944 things had very much moved on since then. This was his first posting as LAC Brown and being regarded as a humble 'erk' didn't faze him at all and he was proud to be associated with the pilots as they lounged around in the dispersal hut. Their charges were single-engine Hawker Typhoon fighters, big, ugly brutes with gaping air intakes to feed their huge Napier Sabre engines.

Keeping the dispersal hut clean and tidy was one of Alf's duties, a task he performed assiduously.

At this late stage of the war, even D-Day seemed to be a distant memory as the squadron awaited a move to France.

One day Alf was hovering in the dispersal, acting as an errand boy when required, when among the hubbub he overheard snatches of a conversation: "…Rhubarb…love more…maybe when we move to France…"

Alf saw a chance to make himself really useful. He'd passed farms on his way here. As nobody wanted anything he slipped away and trudged the couple of miles to the nearest farm which, luck would have it, grew rhubarb.

The farmer was surprised to receive an order for so much rhubarb but on hearing who it was for charged a very low price. Even this took up all Alf's beer and fag money but he didn't mind. Anything for his heroes!

He staggered back to the aerodrome ignoring the odd looks he got from other airmen and at last reached the dispersal hut.

At his entrance, all conversation ceased and two pilots playing chess stopped playing and looked up. "What's all this, Brown?" one of them demanded. Alf stood to attention and awkwardly saluted. He replied:

"I hope you'll forgive me, sir, but I couldn't help overhearing talk about rhubarb. So I've bought some for cookie to make into a crumble or something."

There followed a stunned silence. Then the pilots as one all burst into gales of laughter, then one of them said: "You idiot Brown! After D-Day we were encouraged to fly over enemy lines seeking out targets of opportunity to attack with rockets and cannon, things like tanks, railway engines and convoys. We usually went in pairs. They were great fun and we called them rhubarbs. That's what we were talking about you clot!"

"Oh," said Alf in a small voice and feeing a complete fool.

Another pilot joined in: "The frontline is now too far away for us to reach so we're hoping our move to France will provide more opportunities for rhubarbs."

"Did you get any tea?" queried the first pilot.

"No sir," replied Alf.

The pilot crossed to a cupboard and took out a tin of baked beans. He stuck it under Alf's chin and said: "Take that lot to cookie and see what he can do with it and tell him to make you beans on toast."

To the accompaniment of further gales of laughter Alf headed to the cookhouse. A delicious rhubarb crumble was eventually forthcoming and Alf received a portion.

Henceforth he was known as 'Rhubarb Brown'.

An Amazing Story

Tom pushed his plate away and sighed with contentment. *Not bad for a cheap hotel meal* he thought, then: *Time for a pint or two before I turn in.* He'd noted a little pub a few hundred yards from the hotel so he sallied forth into a very cold evening.

The pub was called 'The Coach and Horses' and Tom was glad to enter out of the cold. Inside were oak beams, horse brasses and a nice open fire. Not much in the way of clientele, but it was a Wednesday. He got himself a pint then took one of the two armchairs either side of the fire, the other being occupied by an old man.

"Cold out tonight," remarked Tom, holding his hands out to the fire. "Ay, that it is," replied the old man. He drained the remains of his pint then went on: "Reminds me of the night I nearly died. I'll never forget that."

Sensing a story coming on, Tom bought the old man a pint then sat down to listen after they'd introduced themselves to each other. The old man – Sam – began:

"I were only about four. We were on holiday in two caravans, my parents, baby Ellie and me in one and Gran and Granddad in the other. One day, we all went to a stately home but after looking round the gardens Gran and Granddad were tired and went. I didn't want to see any old house so I stayed in the garden. Behind a wall I found a great big maze so I went in it. I wandered about with no sense of time, looking for bird's nests in the hedges."

"My parents and Ellie came out and, not seeing me, assumed I had gone with Gran and Granddad as I often did at home. It started to get dark and I found I was lost and couldn't get out. I shouted but the house was too far away for anyone to hear me. I got very scared and cold. No mobile phones in those days."

"It was a clear night with a full moon and it got colder. In the end, I gave up and lay down, wrapping my coat around me. I was soon shivering with chattering teeth and I'm sure I wouldn't have lasted the night. Then I noticed something."

“A cloud had appeared in the sky, lit up by the moon. It was in the shape of a lamb and as I watched it grew bigger. It was coming down on me! But I remembered it was only a cloud and stopped feeling scared. It came right down and I found myself in a mist which was warm! I stopped shivering and went to sleep with this lovely blanket of warmth around me.”

“I awoke to a bright morning, no cloud, and the sound of my dad and mum’s voices calling me. I yelled and they soon found me as they had a guide booklet with a map of the maze in it. Gran and Granddad were with them. I told them my story which made my mum and dad frown as if they didn’t believe me. Gran and Granddad did, especially Gran who said: ‘It was the Lamb of God came down to look after you.’”

Tom listened to the story with interest. It took Sam rather longer to tell it than my writing here during which he sank another two pints and a whisky, all paid for by Tom.

Time to go and Tom left. At the door, he turned and gave a last wave to Sam, standing aside to allow an old lady to pass.

“So you’ve met Sam, ’ave yer?” she said.

“Yes,” replied Tom, “do you know him?”

“Know ’im?” she answered with a grin. “I’ve bin a-married to ’im this last fifty years ’n more. And ’ow many pints did ’e con you out of?” She then passed on into the pub leaving Tom wondering as the light of realisation slowly spread over his face.

All at Sea

Dave Jones loved his boat as did his family of wife, two sons and a daughter. In his eyes, there was nothing lovelier than Sea Queen, all her paint and brass works shining, her snow-white sails unfurled, and no sensation better than when she gently heaved up and down as she furrowed her way through the waves. Every squeak and creak was music to Dave's ears. "She's talking to me," he'd say.

Every winter Sea Queen was taken out of the water when the whole family would pitch in to overhaul and clean her from top to bottom. A 150-year-old sailing ship did look rather incongruous among all the smart motor boats in the marina but Dave didn't care and neither did his family.

There was one person who did. The owner of a smart motor cruiser moored alongside Sea Queen's starboard side. He would shout: "Hey Dave, when 'y gonna buy a proper boat? Can't you afford it?"

"Money is not an issue Brian," Dave would shout back. "We're very happy with Sea Queen and we're keeping her. She's got soul."

"What?" would come an answering shout, "all those sails to heave up and down? Ropes to trip over and relying on the wind?"

"Yes, it is hard work," rejoined Dave, "but the results are well worth it."

"Well you wouldn't catch me on that old tub," said Brian, "and when we go fishing we've caught all the fish before you even get going!"

"We do all right," growled Dave.

The other boat owners viewed these exchanges with detached amusement. They all got on well enough but tended to take Dave's side and to regard Brian as a bit of a bully.

One day, the sea being very choppy, only Dave's and Brian's boats went out. The fishing had been good the previous day. Brian's mate just pressed the starter, cast off and away they went while Dave and family, having to tack from side to side due to on onshore wind, took longer than usual getting out to sea.

They eventually came upon Brian's Dominator boat and Dave was surprised to see everyone clustered around the stern instead of fishing. Brian spotted them and yelled: "Hey, Dave, we're in trouble, can you help?"

Dave hove to and his son dropped anchor. "What's up?" he asked.

"I stupidly left the fuel cap off and sea water's got in," said Brian, "so no engine and no power. We haven't even had a cup of tea. Could you give us a tow?"

"Okay," said Dave.

So it was done. Brian and his crew boarded Sea Queen for a warming cup of tea. On the way back Dave said: "Not such an old tub now, eh?"

"Er – oh, sorry about that," mumbled Brian, then "I'm glad there'll be no one about when we get in."

Dave and his wife, Glenda, looked at each other. Glenda grinned and went below, then quietly spoke into her mobile phone.

When they got in, Brian was dismayed to see quite a crowd on the breakwater who shouted things like: "Elastic band broke, Bri?"

"Good old Wind power!"

"It don't run on water y'know!"

"Take a paddle with you next time!"

Brian never jeered at Sea Queen again.

A Neat Trick

Jack hated the old windmill standing derelict, idle, useless and badly in need of a facelift. As a retired engineer he was only interested in things that worked and were of use. Once they became obsolete they should be re-cycled or dumped in his view. He spent most of his days in his workshop making wooden toys to be sold for charity at the local church fete at Easter or the town gala in August. He also enjoyed mending the toys and bicycles of local children.

His wife Jane, on the other hand, was a staunch defender of the mill as well as being a keen gardener. "Of course, it should be preserved," she'd say, "it's history, heritage and it's high time they spent some money on it."

"Better to knock it down," Jack would reply.

One day anyone of a suspicious nature would have wondered at the sight of Jane and a certain Mr Bartram speaking together in hushed tones in the corner of the post office. An affair or the beginning of one? No, nothing like that. Mr Bartram was a local councillor with a special interest in the mill. He held the keys to it and he kept the lock well oiled.

Over dinner Jane suddenly said: "Oh, by the way, Mr Bartram's starting guided tours of the mill this Sunday."

"Huh, best of luck to him," was Jack's reply.

"I'm going and I want you to come with me," she said firmly.

"Oh, if I must," sighed Jack.

Sunday came and they left early at Jane's insistence. "To avoid the crowds," she said.

Mr Bartram was already there and they all entered the mill, the first time for Jack.

Musty and dusty, he thought as he looked around. He looked at the machinery, gears and shafts all red with rust. He didn't like that. To his engineers mind it was like looking at a dead body.

"You can go upstairs if you like," said Mr Bartram, "it's quite safe."

Jack did so, right to the top, more shafts and gears. He noted some of the gears were made of wood and that one of them was very worn, with missing teeth. *I could make that,* he said to himself, *I wonder how it comes off?* His interest aroused, he looked closer. *I see,* he thought, *You undo that, lower that and knock that wedge out.* He looked out of the small window. The sails seemed in good condition as far as he could tell. Downstairs, two people had their fingers crossed.

Jack came down and looked at the gears and shafts again. They seemed to be in good condition. *Nothing that a wire brush and grease needed,* he thought. Without thinking, he said aloud: "You know, it wouldn't take too much to get this working."

"Oh, really?" said Mr Bartram, "Think you could do it?"

"I'd need help," said Jack.

"No problem there," came the reply, "and I'd be your first volunteer."

Jack stared, and then suspicion dawned. "Hang on," he said. "This was supposed to be a guided tour but we are the only ones here. Where are all the others?"

Mr Bartram and Jane looked at each other then Jane said: "I'm sorry Jack. There's no guided tour. It was a trick to get you here."

"But why?" said Jack with a frown.

Mr Bartram replied. "English Heritage has allotted us funds to restore the mill to working order but we need an engineer. You were the obvious choice."

Jack saw the funny side. "You crafty pair of so and so's." He laughed, then: "But what's the point if it doesn't produce anything?"

"Oh but it will," said Jane. "There are working mills all over the country producing real stone-ground flour. People and especially bakeries love it."

"She's right," interjected Mr Bartram. "You can buy the corn easily enough and there is plenty of information on the internet."

The ploy worked, Jack was hooked and, with much willing help, got stuck in.

The mill was transformed and was soon spruced up and supplying flour to local bakeries, shops and people who still preferred to make their own bread. Jack is never happier when he is presiding over things and Jane looks after the flowers she's planted around it.

Not all tricks are nasty ones!

A Visit

The old man sat on the park bench and thought about his day. He hadn't been back to his old town for a long time – a very long time. His day had started early and he had been amazed at the amount of traffic there was, a constant stream of cars, vans, lorries, buses, motor-cycles and bicycles. He liked the look of the cars, clean, sleek and they didn't smoke like the ones he remembered.

There were things he remembered and expected to see but didn't. Where was the old road sweeper with his barrow? Housewives gossiping over their fences after hanging the washing out? The coal man, the milk man, the bread van and the one with the lady ringing her hand bell as she sold her fish? Ah, there's a postman, at least that hadn't changed.

He noted the people all rushing about wrapped up in themselves with hardly anyone wishing anyone a cheery "Good morning." Not like in his day when it was common practice to do that, even lifting one's hat to a lady.

He went into a small supermarket and noted how ordered and clean everything was, but lacked the cosy friendliness of his old local corner shop and he doubted if this place would allow 'tick'. He was staggered by the prices. Seven quid for a packet of fags? They were less than three bob in his day. And what happened to the money? Pounds but no shillings or pence. He soon realised that the pound was now divided into 100 units so 50 of them would equal 10 shillings. 55p for a Mars bar? Wow, that was eleven bob!

He next looked into the window of a shop selling televisions, very thin things with vast screens, their pictures all in glorious colour. The biggest one cost nearly £1,000 which made him gasp. His first wage had been less than £200 per year!

An estate agent's window was even worse; a king's ransom would be needed to buy a house. He noticed a few shops were boarded up. Not like that in his day, everything seemed to thrive then.

After the best part of the day wandering around, he was amazed at the things he'd seen or not seen. No steam engines for instance and a block of flats where his old school used to be. And what on earth was the internet? People didn't seem so friendly with each other and the old man didn't feel the sense of community he'd known long ago.

So now, late in the afternoon, he sat and looked about him. The duck pond was still there and with ducks on it but no one was feeding them and no couples with small children just strolling about. No one seemed to be playing games as he once had, cricket with a home-made bat and stumps chalked on a wall. Footie with jumpers or coats for goal posts, girls with skipping-ropes. Four old pram wheels and some wood would make a trolley and there were chasing type games that didn't need anything. Running against the wind was one. It was exhausting and one by one a boy or girl would drop out. Last one standing was the winner.

He noted a lot of people of all ages talking into small oblong things they held in their hands. Some sort of radio he supposed. They all looked well fed and affluent. A girl sailed by on roller blades, something else new. He wondered about the wires leading to her ears but of course had no knowledge of the iPod. Then came two boys on skateboards. Like the roller blades they were obviously shop-bought so money didn't appear to be a problem. The boys were both eating sweets from colourful bags marked 'Haribo'. He thought about the sweets from his childhood. Sugar mice displayed in an open tray, very nice but sickly. Betcha can't eat two of them! Liquorice sticks and jelly dummies displayed in the same way. Three pence for a Wagon Wheel or six pence for a bar of chocolate or Palm Toffee. The money for them had to earned by running errands, fags for Mrs Lawes, fish and chips for old Mrs Bolton and the butchers for the even older Mrs Chittenden.

The old man thought it was time to go. He wouldn't be coming back. It was hard to get the special permission and it wasn't worth it. While people seemed to be well off, the old man thought they lacked something – a community soul.

Two girls sat on the bench. The one next to him shivered and said: "Brrr, I went cold then."

"Someone walked over your grave," chuckled the other one.

The old man grinned to himself. He had that effect on people. He then left, back to the other side.

He was a ghost you see.

A Sad Loss

Tommy loved animals but lacked the means to study them properly until one day he spotted a beetle. “Insects,” He said excitedly to himself, “I could study them!”

He began and after a couple of years became, with the invaluable help of his local library, a great expert on his local insect wildlife and always carried a few empty matchboxes with him in case he found a specimen worthy of further study.

One day, he found a beetle on a cabbage in his garden he’d never seen before. He caught it and put it in a matchbox with a piece of cabbage leaf. He showed his dad who said: “You need to show that to the zoo.”

“Yes, I know,” replied Tommy, “but they’ll take it from me so I’ll keep it for a little while.”

Later that day he was walking in the town when he spied his friend Jeff coming out of the sweet shop. “Hey Jeff!” he called, “take a look at this!”

Jeff did and they walked along examining the beetle and sharing Jeff s sweets when they came upon a large pothole at the side of the road. A yellow line had been sprayed around it. “Wow, that’s a really deep one,” remarked Jeff.

Both lads bent over and peered in and they both saw something scuttle into the hole and vanish out of sight. Tommy looked in his matchbox, it was empty! “Oh no!” he wailed, “I must have tilted the box!”

“I’m so sorry,” said Jeff, “what was it called?”

“It didn’t have a name,” said Tommy ruefully, “but I know it was rare so I called it a Rary.”

“Well it’s gone now,” said Jeff, looking down the hole, “and that’s a long was to tip a Rary!”

An Inspiration

Jamie often examined the stained glass window of his local fish and chip shop while he was waiting in the queue to be served. Well, there wasn't much else to look at. He liked the colours and the design in which the main feature was a stylised mermaid playing a guitar. But there was one feature that annoyed him: the guitar.

"She isn't playing it, she's just holding it," he said to himself, "and the guitar has six tuning pegs but only three strings. It doesn't have a tailpiece either. I would have thought the artist could have done better than that."

But Jamie still studied the picture when he visited the shop for his Friday night's supper and one day the seed of an idea began to form in his mind. *Why should I be so critical?* he thought. *After all, I can't play the guitar either.* Then: *I wonder how hard can it be?* The idea grew in his mind until he could hardly think of anything else. Then he decided.

Saturday morning found him in his local music shop. His wage, as a trainee motor mechanic, wasn't high but he took the plunge and, on the advice of the salesman, left the shop with an acoustic guitar in a soft case and a *First Steps into Playing the Guitar* book.

And play he did, surprised and delighted to find he had a natural talent for it, despite very sore fingers.

His elder sister was a leading light in her school choir and began to sing with him. Calling themselves 'The Woodcutters' they began to perform in local pubs and clubs as a clone of the famous 'Carpenters'. After a while, they began to compose their own songs and were one day spotted by a record company executive who had popped into the pub for a quick one where they happened to be playing.

One thing led to another and eventually Jamie and Ethel achieved world-wide fame!

Inspiration can come from anywhere!

Not for Girls

It was a laborious climb, especially for a man of his age. But he was determined to make it as he was the last of them.

Pausing often to catch his breath and trying to ignore the pain in his joints and arthritic fingers, he slowly ascended. He knew he would never reach the top but didn't intend to, he just wanted to reach the place where they all used to sit and eat their crisps and Mars bars and drink their Tizer.

He finally reached it, removed the knapsack from his back, set it down and, with a sigh of relief, sat down. He looked out to sea, a view he hadn't seen from this vantage point for many decades. His mind wandered back over all those years to a time long past.

There had been six of them, boys all born in the same small town who had grown up together. They were just typical lads, loud, boisterous with much energy which they dissipated by spending as much time outdoors as possible. In the manner of William Brown and his Outlaws, books they all loved and immortally invented by Richmal Crompton, they formed themselves into a close-knit gang they called the 'Mavericks'.

They formalised a set of rules. Mavericks would always be true to one another, would always help one another, would not divulge their secrets to anyone else and would always keep in touch with one another wherever they may be as adults. There would be no leader and, most important of all, the Mavericks were not for girls who were regarded as sissy, giggling creatures, totally unsuited for games of soldiers etc.

One day the Mavericks were playing in some bushes about three miles from home when they found The Rock. Of course they had to climb it and from henceforth it became their centre of operations. The old man grinned as he remembered.

They used to race each other up and down it or, with blackened faces, pretend to be SAS men, creeping silently upwards towards an unseen enemy and communicating only with grimaces and gestures. Other times they would stand on the top when the rock would become a fortress and they would hurl down imaginary rocks and boiling oil down on an equally imaginary enemy. The rock could also be a ship which they defended against pirates or saw the Spanish Armada coming when there would be cries of: "bring up the powder!" and "load the guns!" One of the lads was given a decent telescope through which they took turns watching passing ships.

One game they used to play was that of making up stories about the ships and the old man laughed aloud when he remembered his and how the others had laughed at it. In it, a small ship carrying a cargo of balloons was wrecked on a desert island and all the crew killed. The natives thought the balloons were personal adornments and many were the howls of anguish when they tried to wear them in the manner of condoms!

The years passed and the Mavericks grew up and went their separate ways. But they kept in touch and kept their secrets. One by one they passed away until only the old man was left.

It was time. The old man opened his knapsack and took out a single-use barbecue, a bottle and a paper packet which he opened to reveal a piece of steak. He got the barbecue alight and placed the steak on it then, using the corkscrew attachment of his Swiss Army knife, uncorked the bottle.

He held the bottle up to the sun and shouted: "Good luck lads wherever you are!" then took a good swig out of the bottle before putting it down again.

After ensuring the barbecue was well alight and there was no foliage anywhere near the old man slowly descended and made his way home.

His wife opened the door. "Where on earth have you been?" she said, "The girls are here."

Sure enough their two grown-up daughters were sitting at the kitchen table. "We were worried, Dad," said one. "You could've let us know," said the other.

"It's not for girls," said the old man as he removed his knapsack and sank gratefully into a chair. His wife looked into the knapsack.

"It's empty," she said, "and what do you mean 'it's not for girls'?"

"That's all I can say," replied the old man. "It's not for girls and I can't say any more."

The three women looked at each other. Was he going gaga? But he wasn't and life went on.

By and by, the old man passed on and the Mavericks were no more.

So if you happen to come across the rock and feel inclined to climb it you may find the bottle and the remains of the barbecue still there. Please don't touch them; they're a memorial you see.

A Toothy Tale

“I’m sorry boys,” said Beryl as she looked up from the paper, “it’s not looking good for tomorrow.” Her husband Danny rose from his chair, went to the barometer that hung in the hall, and tapped it.

“She’s right,” he said, “rain is coming.”

Their two teenage sons groaned. They had saved their pocket money all month to pay for a good session on the new open-air Go Kart track which had opened recently a couple of miles away.

The next day, Saturday, increased their gloom still further. It was raining all right, not the heavy stuff which might indicate a passing shower or the very light tolerable drizzle but a steady downpour and no wind to blow it away.

So the boys and their parents sat around, Beryl knitting, Danny struggling with a crossword while the boys lounged about bored as they checked the rain every few minutes.

Then Danny decided to at least try to relieve the air of despondency. He said: “We were talking at work last week and Bill reminded me of that comedy we used to watch called ‘Alas Smith and Jones’ with Mel Smith and Griff Rhys Jones.”

“The sketch was a funeral with Jones as the vicar and Smith as a mourner. Then Smith’s hat falls off into the grave so Jones stops the service. Smith goes down to get his hat but his foot goes through the lid of the coffin so there he is wearing it like a big surfboard. He gets it off, gets out and the service resumes.”

“Then there is a ‘clunk’. It’s Smith’s spectacles this time. Jones, with a frown, again stops the service and with many apologies Smith retrieves them, damaging the coffin lid a bit more. The service resumes.”

Beryl and the boys are now all ears, awaiting the punch line. Danny continues:

“Then a second ‘clunk’ is heard. Jones, getting a bit irritated, says: ‘What is it now?’”

“My false teeth,” replied Smith, “sorry.”

“So down he goes again and soon emerges with a toothy grin on his face and more apologies.”

“The service resumes once more but Jones notices Smith is pulling faces and frowning. ‘Is something the matter?’ he asks. ‘These are not my teeth!’ says Smith.”

“Oh God!” said the elder son, “you mean he got them off the—?”

“Yuk!” said the younger one, “that’s horrible!”

Danny and Beryl laugh then she says: “Yes, but it’s funny. It reminds me of when I worked as an auxiliary night nurse in a geriatric ward. We had 34 patients and nearly all of them had false teeth which had to be cleaned last thing every night. It was not a popular job so we got the junior nurses to do it.”

“So one night we got this new girl to do the job and later she was found by the ward sister in the sink room with a tooth brush and a bowl full of teeth.”

“‘You idiot!’ said the sister, ‘you’re supposed to clean them individually. How do you know which teeth belong to which patient?’”

“The girl burst into tears but Sister was having none of that. ‘You can stop that’ she said. ‘Finish cleaning them then sort them out in the morning.’”

“Well, we helped as did the day staff but it still took most of the next day to sort it all out.”

The others laughed then Danny looked out and said: “Hey boys, you’re in luck, the rain’s stopped.”

The boys rushed for their coats and bicycles and one of them said: “Did you clean your teeth this morning?”

“’Course I did,” came the reply, “why?”

“Well, I’m going to make sure I clean mine regularly,” said his brother, “I don’t want to end up with false ones!”

A Small War

Victor had been serving a group of local villages as their postie for nearly 15 years and knew most people by their names. He wasn't looking forward to his last call. This was not previously the case as Mr and Mrs Francois always welcomed him with a couple of croissants and a cup of coffee, very welcome on a cold day. He always made them his last call even if he didn't have any mail for them.

Mr Francois was French while his wife was English. They had met before the war in France but now their long and happy marriage had ended with the sudden death of Mr Francois. Mrs Francois had been away with relatives after the funeral but now she was home and Victor had two letters for her.

She looked pretty normal when she opened the door, a bit sad of course. She invited Victor in and there were the croissants waiting for him, one cheese and bacon, the other chocolate. He sat down and expressed his condolences while she poured the coffee.

"Well at least I can tell the story now," she said suddenly, causing Victor to look up.

"Story?" he queried.

"Jacques wouldn't tell anyone." she said. "He thought they might want him again one day."

"Want him?" said a puzzled Victor, "Who?"

"The British Secret Service," she replied. "I'll tell you about it." Victor sat back all ears as he demolished his croissants and coffee. So Mrs Francois began:

"We met before the war. He worked on the railways and rose to become an inspector. We never had children. We lived in a little place called Massy which is on the outskirts of Paris. His job meant he had to travel around to other stations, sorting out problems, making reports, ensuring timetables were adhered to and checking out proposed new ones. He sometimes brought work home with him. Hang on a minute."

She went to the sideboard and brought out an old briefcase and a threadbare jacket which smelt strongly of mothballs and had the word 'Inspecteur' embroidered on both lapels. She resumed:

"Others besides Churchill knew the war was coming and one day two men called, one French, the other English. They wanted my husband to work for them, supplying information such as troop movements, rail disruption etc. – assuming the Germans invaded, of course. Jacques readily agreed although I wanted to come to England. 'I stay for France' he would say so of course I stayed with him."

"A radio was duly supplied and to hide it he built an air raid shelter in the garden with a hidden cupboard in one corner and his hobby, which I'll tell you about later." Victor listened, fascinated.

"Well, the war came and he was kept busy relaying as much information as possible, gathered as he travelled around the network, usually by rail but sometimes by car. Dunkirk came and went and the Germans occupied us. We went to Paris to see them marching in and Hitler smiling all over his silly face."

"Resistance was set up and Jacques relayed messages and requests to and from them. He never stayed on the radio long which prevented the Boche from getting a fix on his transmissions. Things stayed pretty calm until D-Day when all hell broke loose. Jacques was kept very busy with his job and his radio. He was often stopped by the Gestapo and his briefcase – this one – examined but they found only timetables, schedules and stuff like that. The messages and codes he carried back and forth were in here." And so saying she turned the collar of the jacket and said: "Run your fingers along the stitching there." Victor did so and found his fingers slipping inside. A hidden pocket! "Wow," he said, "that's brilliant!"

"I made it," came the reply. She went on: "We got raided but they never found the radio and here's why – the best bit."

"Jacque's hobby was a flea circus which he kept in a large glass case on a trestle table in the air raid shelter. One day three Germans came to search our house, a junior officer and two privates. They found nothing of course so went out into the garden. The officer, who spoke French said: 'Ah, an air raid shelter' as they walked towards it, 'what do you keep in there?'"

"Nothing," replied Jacques, "except my fleas."

"Fleas?" exclaimed the officer, coming to a dead stop and at the same time flinging out both arms to stop his men, "what fleas?"

“Jacques explained his hobby and said that he was always on the lookout for more fleas because some of them died, which was true, and some of them escaped, which was not true, but the squeaky-clean German didn’t know that.”

“‘We go,’ he said and they did and never came back and that was how fleas helped us win the war!’ ‘What a great story,’ said Victor, ‘and great memories too.’ ‘Yes,’” came the reply. “Jacques never replaced the fleas as they died, the war ended, he handed the radio in and we retired here, leaving the empty case in the air raid shelter.”

A Musical Interlude

Ken loved the saxophone. It had all started when he was given a toy one for his sixth birthday. It had eight notes – a complete octave – and was more or less in tune. Ken soon learned a selection of simple tunes. With the help of the little book that came with it, he soon learned the names of the notes and could name any one of them just by hearing them.

At the age of eleven, he went up to a secondary modern school where they had music lessons. Recorders were supplied which Ken quickly mastered. He progressed rapidly and the teacher noted his enthusiasm, talent and great interest in the saxophone. He had a word with Ken's parents. "He needs some one-to-one teaching," he said. "He has the makings of a top musician. I know someone who gives lessons and plays the saxophone."

So it was arranged for Ken to go and, to his great delight, got his hands on a real saxophone.

He took to it like a duck to water even though his twelve and a half year old fingers found it hard to reach some of the keys. His fourteenth birthday came and went but the saxophone he was given stayed, to his great joy. His very own!

As he practiced, which he did often, his two elder sisters would walk around making 'honk, honk' and 'parp, parp' noises so Ken decided to practice elsewhere. He rode on his bicycle to a small pond he knew of about two miles away.

He rode round it to where he knew there was an old concrete boundary marker and a few tree stumps. It was quiet and peaceful here with only the odd passer-by who invariably stopped to listen then walked on. He sat on the marker and played.

When he was nineteen, Ken won a scholarship to a school of music. This meant living away from home but with his grant, help from his parents and the odd gig with a local band he was able to afford a small car.

Weekends found him back home with his family. His sisters no longer mocked, if fact one was married and gone. Now he drove to the pond and walked round to the stone carrying his saxophone and a cool box with sandwiches and cans of drink in it. It was still his favourite place to practice.

One day he became aware of movement to his left. He slightly turned his head without removing his mouthpiece. A girl. She sat on a tree stump, her bicycle propped against the other side. Ken continued, she didn't move.

Finally he stopped and said: "Hello." She grinned with a "Hi, I like your playing."

"Oh, thanks," replied Ken.

They soon began to chat and she told him her name was Rose and she had recently moved into the area with her parents and brother. Ken told her he'd be there again the next Sunday, weather permitting, as they shared his sandwiches and cold drink.

Ken spent the next week in a state of excitement. Would she turn up? Unbeknownst to him, Rose was thinking the same thing!

So the two began to see a lot of each other and in the fullness of time became engaged. Rose was training to be a primary school teacher so she had her studies too.

Time passed, in its inexorable way, and one day Ken's tutor took him to one side and said: "I have a friend who plays sax in the Ray Burns orchestra. He's retiring soon and I could put in a good word for you. I think you'd have a good chance, you're certainly good enough."

Ken nearly leapt up into the air! Ray Burns! Wow! A dream come true!

Needless to say Ken got the job and a great career followed. Concerts, dances and providing the backing to many famous singers on stage, television and in the recording studio. Rose followed her own career but the two still found time to get married, buy a house some distance away and produce two boys.

Jumping ahead many years we find Ken and Rose both retired and enjoying life together, their normal peaceful existence only pleasantly broken by the visits of their children and grandchildren. Ken's saxophone rested in its case in the sideboard. He didn't play anymore and he and Rose's enjoyment of music was confined to listening to it.

Then came the terrible day when Ken lost Rose. A short burst of very virulent cancer and a mercifully quick end. Ken was devastated even though the boys and their families were a great comfort. He carried on alone for a few years, keeping the bungalow and garden tidy.

One day, Ken removed the saxophone from the sideboard and took it out of its case. How familiar it felt in his hands! Some of the valves, in common with his fingers, were a bit stiff. He replaced it in its case and carried to his car, then drove the 20 odd miles to the pond and parked. He was surprised to see it had dried up. He walked round to the stone. The tree stump had rotted and crumbled to his touch.

He sat down and began to play as well as his stiff fingers and the valves would allow. In his mind's eye, he saw Rose sitting there in a flowery dress, her hands demurely in her lap, a rapt expression on her face and the slight breeze ruffling her hair. *Mustn't get sad,* he said to himself.

At last, it was time to go. Ken was getting cold. He went with one last look at the stone and the stump, mute witnesses to the events of so long ago. Ken wished he could go back and do it all again but he knew that the road of life is only one way and there is no return ticket.

Back home Ken turned on the electric fire and had a warming tot of whisky. He then thoroughly cleaned his saxophone and applied tiny drops of oil to its valves before replacing it in its case and then in the sideboard. He then settled down in his armchair with his memories.

That was how they found him in the morning. Heart attack, the doctor said. There followed a period of grief, a funeral and the disposal of the bungalow and its contents.

Except for the saxophone. That stayed in the family and was never played again.

Seek and Ye Shall Find

"I'm sorry Mrs Jones," said Mr Shaw, taking off his cap and scratching his head. "You need to spend £3,500 now if you are to avoid a whole new roof in a few years' time."

"I don't have that sort of money," replied the old lady from the depths of her armchair, "and Nora can't help, not with those two boys to bring up and George the only breadwinner. They don't own their own house anyway."

"You could sell up," said Mr Jones. "There are firms who buy your house while you continue to live in it and then when you, ahem, go if the value of the house is greater than the loan plus interest the balance goes to your next of kin."

"Oh no," said Mrs Jones indignantly, "I'm not doing that. I promised the house to Nora which is what my will says."

"Well, I'll leave you to it then," said Mr Jones replacing his cap. "Sorry, it wasn't better news." And with that he left.

Mrs Jones then reached for the phone, looked up a number in a little book and dialled it. "Frank?" she asked when there was an answer, "Ada Jones here. Can you come round? I need to raise some money."

'Frank' was Frank Bellamy or 'Fair Deal Frank' as he liked to style himself. He was a local dealer who also carried out house clearances. "Treat 'em fair and they'll come back," was his motto.

He duly arrived and after the usual pleasantries began to look around the bungalow.

"That Clarice Cliff tea set looks good," he said at last, "could be £800 or more there."

"I'm not selling that," retorted Mrs Jones, "it was a wedding present and anyway, I need a lot more than £800."

Frank then noticed some CDs stacked on a cabinet. "Elvis fan I see," he remarked.

“Oh yes,” smiled Mrs Jones. “Bert was too. He had one of those auto-changer things which often dropped two records instead of one and you had to turn the records over of course. CDs are much more convenient. I chucked the auto-changer out years ago.”

Frank looked again at the cabinet. Lots of very shallow drawers. A coin cabinet and a pretty expensive one. *Somebody must've had a good coin collection to justify this,* he thought as he pulled a drawer open. Its compartments were full of buttons, pins, needles, thimbles, hooks, eyes and many reels of different coloured cotton.

“That's my sewing stuff,” said Mrs Jones who was watching him. “Can't do much these days 'cos of the arthritis but I can still do a bit.”

“Where did the cabinet come from?” asked Frank.

“It was Bert's,” she replied, “He kept his old coins in it.”

Frank was almost afraid to ask the next question. Had the coins gone the way of the auto-changer?

“What happened to the coins?” he said at last.

“They're up in the attic,” came the reply. “Come to think of it they're silver, maybe worth something? If you want to look you'll need to get the step ladder out of the shed. I haven't been up there for years.” Then she added: “His records are up there too. There is a light but I can't remember where the switch is now.”

Frank fetched the step ladder and placed it under the hatch. He climbed up, pushed the hatch cover out of the way and fumbled around until he found the switch. Mrs Jones stood next to the ladder and said: “Do take care. All Bert's stuff is in a box with broken hinges.”

The attic had been partially floored and Frank quickly reached and removed the lid from a large wooden box which stood close to the hatch.

The first item inside was a model aeroplane with a broken wing, all flimsy balsa wood and tissue paper full of holes. Frank remembered these and the smell of dope. They took ages to make and more ages to wind the elastic up by twirling the propeller with the forefinger. The resultant flight was disappointedly short and often ended with a splintering crash. Frank removed it.

Next a heap of old ‘Coin & Medal’ magazines and a large, heavy plastic bag. Frank looked inside and his eyes widened. Records on the Sun label! The studio where Elvis started his recording career before he went to RCA! Frank had a quick look. All Elvis' early stuff plus some Johnny Cash, Jerry Lee Lewis and Carl Perkins and all in Sun's garish paper sleeves! *There's money here,* thought

Frank, *collectors will go mad.* Then he spotted an old shoe box which was pleasingly heavy when he picked it up. A peek under the lid revealed coins!

He replaced the aeroplane and the box lid then placed the carrier bag and the shoe box close to the hatch. Then he made two trips to get them down, switched the light off, replaced the hatch cover and returned the step ladder to the shed. Then over a cup of tea he and Mrs Jones examined the coins which she had placed in layers on tissue paper in the shoe box. They were all large silver coins, some blackened but Frank knew better than to clean them. There were British crowns from several reigns, a good selection of American silver dollars, another of 8 reales, the famed 'pieces of eight' from several South American countries, thalers from Austria and others Franks didn't recognise. "Would you want to get rid of these?" he asked.

"Yes," said Mrs Jones, "I've got my CDs and the coins never interested me. Only the ones I could spend." She added with a laugh.

It's easy to guess the rest. Two separate specialist auctions paid for Mrs Jones' roof and gave her a decent building society account for the first time in her life.

Interesting places attics, you never know what you might find!

One Good Turn

Brookdene was a small village of about 25 houses situated on a rise above a road that separated it from the river Dene. It was surrounded on three sides by farmland which suited the residents because it meant greedy property developers couldn't extend the village. The opposite side of the river was farmland too. A few of the residents worked but most were retired and they included what most saw as the fly in the ointment as it were – Henry.

Henry was a keen collector of militaria, housing his collection, with its attendant books, in the garage as his wife Mary preferred not to have any of them in the house.

This meant that their sole means of transport was parked on the short, sloping drive and it was this that was the main bone of contention. It was an ex-army Austin Champ, a Jeep-like vehicle which had taken most of Henry's savings to buy and, with the help of the Military Vehicle Society, he could just about afford to run. Its paintwork was in a very faded and dull condition prompting comments such as: "Eyesore!" or "Why don't you get a proper car?" But Henry couldn't afford to get it professionally restored and for that reason never entered it in the *War and Peace* show he attended each year in Kent, leaving it in a far corner of the car park. Then the flood changed everything.

The village had never seen rain like it. The river had never overflowed its banks before but now it did with a vengeance. As the water rose the villagers moved their cars up onto their sloping drives, but its depth became such that they were marooned. Enter Henry and the Champ which was designed to cope with such conditions.

It took five days for the water to subside to manageable levels and during that time the Champ became the villager's sole means of transport. Henry ran people to and from work and with Mary did shopping for others. He even ran one or two to the town doctor's for appointments. He refused all payments, to the consternation of his wife.

One day, when it was all over, three men knocked at Henry's door. Upon being admitted, they announced that they represented a very grateful village and every adult in it had contributed to having the Champ restored. A restorer had been found, photographs sent, an estimate received and the money paid so Henry had no choice in the matter. There were plenty of offers to supply transport for Henry and his wife while the Champ was away. Henry could only gape and stammer his thanks while his smiling wife Mary, who'd known about this all along, looked on.

In due course, an ex-army lorry arrived towing a trailer onto which the Champ was loaded. After plenty of tea and militaria-based chat plus a tour of Henry's collection, the Champ was borne away to its temporary home.

Weeks passed. Then one day the lorry, trailer and Champ reappeared at Henry's door. Henry almost cried when he saw how the faded Champ had been turned into a thing of utilitarian beauty. The correct shade of paint and unit markings, it looked brand new! Henry couldn't wait until the next *War and Peace* show.

When it came Henry, together with Mary this time, attended. No longer was the Champ hidden in a corner of the car park, it was entered into the show where it won the 'Best in Class' award. Henry thought he'd burst with pride!

Back home there were no further jibes from villagers. Their grandchildren loved riding in the Champ and helping to clean it.

Yes, one good turn deserves another!

A Quick Decision

Hamid frowned. There they were again blocking his car in. Luckily, he wasn't going anywhere today. He blamed his neighbour Jalid Hussein who did nothing to discourage the youths who fluttered round his two pretty teenage daughters like flies round honey, leaving their scooters parked all over the road with their steering locked so Hamid couldn't move them. He'd got fed up with having to knock on Jalid's door to ask them to move.

Sometimes the four youths and the two girls would hang around outside, laughing and chattering like so many chirping birds. On being asked to move, the boys would say: "Immediately, Mr Singh," and would move their scooters, only to put them back the next time.

Hamid's own children were younger. Soraya was just past her ninth birthday and his son Omid was coming up to five.

One day Hamid emerged with a bucket and sponge with the intention of washing his car. The six youngsters lounged outside chattering and drinking soft drinks from cans.

Suddenly there was a scream, causing everybody to look up. Hamid's wife Laleh came running out. "It's Soraya!" she cried, "She's drunk from a bottle of white spirit thinking it was lemonade! She needs hospital quickly!"

Hamid put the bucket down and said: "Bring her out, I will take her now." And to the boys: "Move now, please."

One of the boys, Habib, said: "Mr Singh, you'll never get through the traffic, let us take her."

Hamid hesitated. He knew all about Tehran's city streets, a cacophony of hooting and shouting from innumerable cars, buses, lorries, taxis, scooters, motor-cycles, bicycles, pedestrians and vendors selling all sorts of things and everybody getting in each other's way with no semblance of order.

Habib saw his hesitation and said urgently: "You need to decide now, Mr Singh, time is pressing."

Laleh appeared holding Soraya who was clutching her stomach with a face contorted in pain. At this sight, Hamid's mind was made up. He said: "Okay, you take her. Laleh you stay and look after Omid."

"Get her behind me," ordered Habib. "She can hold on to my belt. Eman, you take Mr Singh, Khalid, Ahman, you lead the way."

So the little convoy set off. The two solo scooters leading with their riders sounding their horns, waving one arm or the other and shouting: "Emergency! Make way!" as they all snaked and weaved from left to right through the traffic and dust. On any other occasion, Hamid would have had his heart in his mouth as the saying goes, but his concern for Soraya precluded any such thoughts.

They reached the hospital where a crying Soraya was quickly whisked away by the staff. Hamid and the boys adjourned to the waiting room where they sat and he paced up and down.

A last a white-coated figure appeared with the badge of a doctor, a stethoscope, around her neck. She was smiling. "Soraya will be okay now," she said. "We've pumped her stomach out. She will be a bit sore for a while as white spirit has a drying effect. We'll keep her in for a couple of days then she'll be fine. She's sleeping now, luckily you got her here quickly."

Hamid thanked her, called Laleh on his mobile with the good news, then thanked the boys profusely. "You will all come for a meal with us," he said, which was a traditional gesture of Iranian hospitality.

The journey home was more sedate with Hamid marvelling at the skill of the riders. The two girls were still outside awaiting news.

In due course, Soraya returned home none the worse and shyly thanked the boys. The meal was arranged and enjoyed by the two families and the boys.

All this made Hamid look at scooters in a different light. They were much better in traffic, cheaper to run and less polluting than a car. His journeys to and from work were always alone and he'd actually enjoyed the ride back from the hospital.

Thus Hamid became yet another member of the two-wheeled fraternity, his car being reserved for family outings. He was able to get to and from work much quicker saving him half an hour each way. Another convert!

The Sting

Jamie was teaching himself to play the piano. At a mere five-and-a-half-years-old, he wasn't doing too well. No child prodigy here! The piano was a hand-me-down, neither of his parents played.

Jamie took a bite out of the pork pie his mother had supplied then replaced it on the plate which sat on top of the piano. He stared at the piece of music in front of him with a distinct lack of understanding. He knew the notes between the lines were FACE and those on the lines, EGBDF, could be remembered by the mnemonic 'Every Good Boy Deserves Fun'. With a sigh, he went back to playing the only tune he knew – 'Chopsticks'.

A few minutes passed. Jamie absent-mindedly reached again for his pork pie, not knowing that an inquisitive bee had decided to explore it.

The bee resented the intrusion and showed it by stinging Jamie. Unlike wasps, bees cannot withdraw their stings and the sight of this one stuck to his hand plus the accompanying pain caused Jamie to scream. His parents came running and Dad quickly knocked the bee off, killed it and put it in the waste bin while mother gently withdrew the sting, leaving a tearful Jamie still in pain.

The pain gradually went away but Jamie's fear of bees didn't. In fact, it became something of an obsession, especially during the summer and autumn months. During these times he didn't want to play in the garden, help with a barbecue, play outside with his friends or go on a picnic. If he did participate in any of these things, he spent most of his time there anxiously scanning the sky for any sign of a bee and panicking if he saw one.

School was the same. The playground and the sports field were not his favourite places. No problem in the winter of course, no bees about then. Jamie's parents hoped he'd grow out of it, but he didn't. Then fate lent a hand.

When Jamie was coming up to nine years old, he came home from school one day bursting with excitement. "Mum! Dad!" he cried, "I've had a brilliant day!"

"Oh? What happened?" asked his mum. The response came out in a rush:

"We learnt all about how honey is made and after lunch we went to this sort of garden where there were lots of little white hutch things. We had to wear a white suit and boots and gloves and a funny white hat with net all over it and the man had a smoke thing."

Jamie paused for breath, then: "The man took the lid off one of the hutches and squirted smoke inside then he lifted out a big thing called a honeycomb which was fantastic, all full of little compartments called cells, there were hundreds of them and you can get honey from them. Imagine having free honey in your garden! Could we do it?" And with that he produced a small pot of golden honey from his satchel. "They gave each one of us this," he said proudly, holding it up.

Jamie's parents were flabbergasted and stared at him in amazement. "But the bees," his father at last ventured to say, "weren't you scared?"

"Oh no," said Jamie, "not any more. Not now I've seen how we can get free honey from them." He was cured!

But it didn't end there. With the aid of library books and the internet, Jamie learnt all about beekeeping and as a teenager was able to supply his family with his own bees' honey.

It didn't end there either. As an adult Jamie expanded his operation into a full scale commercial enterprise, selling his honey to a large conglomerate which blended and marketed the products from many beekeepers. Jamie derived a useful income from this plus free honey for his family and a hobby he loved, calling his bees 'my busy little lovelies'.

Sometimes children visited who would invariably ask: "You aren't afraid of being stung?"

"No," Jamie would reply. "But I was once!"

Impasse

The villages of North Tilston and South Tilston stood on either side of a shallow stream crossed by a small bridge of indeterminate age. The chairman of North Tilston Parish Council was carpet fitter Bert Hopkins who was married to Agnes. His opposite number at South Tilston Parish Council was seller of garden supplies Gordon Danby who was married to Joan. Things were peaceful enough in the two villages until day they weren't.

On that day, the two men waved goodbye to their respective wives, two faces at two windows, and climbed into their respective small pick-up trucks.

Bert was going to a house in South Tilston to deliver and fit a carpet in accordance with the wishes of the householder while Gordon intended to deliver several bags of compost to a waiting householder in North Tilston.

They met on the bridge which was not wide enough to allow two vehicles to pass each other. Two heads popped out of two cab windows and Bert began the following exchange:

"Back up, then."

"No, you back up, I was here first."

"No, you wasn't."

"Yes, I was."

"You're closer to your end of the bridge."

"No, I'm not."

"Well, we'll soon see about that!"

And with that Bert got out of his truck and from his tool box in the back removed a large tape measure. Upon seeing this, Gordon got out too. They measured the distance from the middle of Bert's front wheel to his end of the bridge, then repeated it with Gordon's front wheel. Both measurements were the same, so Bert initiated another exchange:

"You should defer to me because I'm older than you."

"Only four years." Then as an afterthought: "My truck's older than yours!"

"Trucks don't count, they're not people."

"Okay then, I'll toss you for it."

Bert having agreed Gordon produced a 50p coin. "You call," he said as he flicked the coin into the air.

"Heads," said Bert as the coin, twinkling in the sun, descended. It bounced off the parapet with a 'ping' and dropped into the stream. Both men looked over. It wasn't very high and they could see the coin in the clear water. "Its tails!" exulted Gordon, "You have to back up!"

"Oh no," retorted Bert. "You were supposed to catch it, not let it fall into the water! That doesn't count."

Then the bridge intervened. While it was quite strong enough to bear the weight of a single truck passing over it, the dead weight of two trucks at its centre was a different matter and it voiced its displeasure by the emitting of a loud CRACK! Fear swept over the two men's faces and, as one, they turned and ran to their respective ends of the bridge to the great amusement of two small knots of spectators as both were not a little overweight. They just made it as with a loud CRASH! The bridge dumped itself together with the two trucks into the stream.

The noise brought more people out of their houses including the two wives.

"What's happened here?" Asked Agnes upon sighting the trucks perched on the rubble.

"It was 'im!" Shouted Bert, "we were both on the bridge and 'e wouldn't back up!"

"No it wasn't!" Gordon shouted back, "we tossed for it and 'e lost and wouldn't 'ave it. That's my 50p in the water!"

"You stupid pair of lummoxes!" scolded Agnes, "hang on, Joan, I'm coming over." And with that she stepped down the low bank and waded across the stream, picking up Gordon's 50p on the way and throwing it to him.

Once she was across and up the opposite bank, the two wives went off into a huddle while their husbands walked up and down alternatively staring glumly at their trucks and glaring at each other.

The two wives re-appeared. Agnes spoke: "Right," she said determinedly with arms folded. "This is what will happen. You two will pay to have the trucks removed and repaired and you will both pay to have the bridge rebuilt. Then your respective councils will sanction the erection of traffic lights on the bridge which is something they should have done years ago. Until it is all done there will be no special favours and certainly no rumpy-pumpy."

Joan piped up: "And don't think the kids are going to be running errands for you either!" Bert blushed bright red.

"Rumpy-pumpy?" he queried, "Dunno what you're talking about." While Gordon suddenly developed a severe cough and all to the laughter and applause from the two groups of onlookers.

And so it was all done. The trucks were removed and repaired causing quite big dents in Bert's and Gordon's finances and the re-building of the bridge caused even bigger ones. The traffic lights duly appeared and peace settle once more upon the two villages. Bert and Gordon soon forgot all about it and resumed the friendship they had enjoyed before.

So, once again, the common sense of women prevailed over the stubborn pig-headedness of men.

A Very Lucky Find

It is no fun being unemployed. Colin had been thus for nearly four months and time was weighing very heavily on his mind. Money was tight too. Luckily his wife, Jane, had a decent job which covered the mortgage. Their two girls helped where they could but such help was necessarily limited as they both had their own lives, houses and marriages to run. Colin's gammy leg, the result of a childhood accident, and his sub-standard eyesight didn't help as that meant he couldn't drive and was only suited to office work. His last job had been such a one, but a change of ownership, reorganisation and a slimming down of staff meant he and some others were out. The few thousand redundancy pay he'd been given was salted away in the building society. Well, he had to have something to boost his old age pension. At his present age of 57 that wasn't too far away.

Colin spent most of his days walking. It kept him fit and, together with his stick, helped his bad leg. Today he walked out to the woods which he knew like the back of his hand. *I'll go up as far as the old cottage,* he thought.

The lonely cottage had been derelict for years. Colin vaguely remembered the old man who'd lived there, a recluse who kept himself to himself and didn't encourage visitors. No one claimed the cottage after he'd died and it had gradually fallen into a dilapidated state, not helped by the vandalism such places invariably attract.

Colin reached the cottage at last and leant on the wall next to a broken window. He noticed the overflowing dustbin its contents, due to the lack of a lid, reduced to a pulpy mass by rain.

Colin idly looked in at the broken window and noted the dust dancing in the sunbeams which streamed in through a second broken widow, broken glass on the floor and old letters strewn about. Otherwise, the room was empty.

The front door stood open and Colin, on an impulse, went in although he'd never bothered to do so on any of his many previous visits to the cottage. He picked up a letter, blew the dust from it and saw it was only an old bill for coal addressed to ‘Mr J. Wilkins’. “So that was the old man’s name,” Colin said to himself. The name Wilkins rang a faint bell somewhere but he couldn’t think where. He turned to leave but as he did so he noticed a piece of wallpaper which had detached itself from the wall and hung forlornly down. Then he noticed something else. The corner of a paper behind the wallpaper. Colin pulled it out. No wonder the wallpaper had peeled from the wall; it wasn’t stuck at that point.

What he was holding was an old manuscript. It had been written in a very spidery hand which, apart from a few ‘thees’ and ‘thous’, Colin couldn’t read. The title was plain: ‘A Concoction’ as was the signature: ‘Josiah Wilkins’. Colin pocketed the paper and returned home.

At home, he was delighted to find his eldest daughter, Jennifer, there. “Hello Jenny,” he said, “what brings you here?”

“I brought some veggies out of our garden for you and Mum,” she replied, pointing to a bulging bag on the floor. “I’m glad to put that down. Cup of tea?”

“Thanks and yes please,” he replied as she moved towards the kitchen.

“And where have you been?” she asked. So he told her and showed her the paper. She looked at it and gasped.

“They’ve been looking for this for years,” she said, “it was in the papers about a year ago. I think this is the original recipe for Wildberryade which was owned by the Wilkins family until about 50 years ago when they sold out. It hasn’t been seen for over a hundred years.”

Colin was very familiar with Wildberryade. Two bottles of it stood in the larder. A very popular soft drink worldwide, earning big profits for its owners and shareholders.

The owners were quickly contacted who soon confirmed that the paper was the missing original recipe (they only had a copy). They were overjoyed to get it and were happy to pay Colin a very substantial reward and, learning of his plight, offered him a job! Colin accepted of course.

This was with the proviso that neither Colin nor any member of his family divulged the contents of the recipe. This was fine because none of them could read the spidery handwriting anyway!

A Varied Day

Masie had a busy morning ahead of her. What with Cyril's birthday on Saturday she had baking to do plus his cake to mix and bake too. Also the new TV aerial is due to come today which would be a great relief, she and Cyril had had big problems with their puny indoor aerial and small, rather dated, TV set. There is always such a lot to be organised when you move into your first house. *Thank goodness we're away from my parents,* she thought.

A new television had been bought as well, a huge 55 inch, thin rectangle; it sat in the corner awaiting the signal from afar that would bring it to life.

The morning wore on. Masie rolled pastry, mixed ingredients and perspired in the heat of the kitchen. The TV man came with his ladders, cable, aerial and satellite dish and got on with installing the latter two items.

At last, Masie was done. The cake was in the oven and the sausage rolls all packed away in their tin. Other items such as sandwiches and trifle would be made later. Just the washing-up to do. Masie was soon immersed in hot water and washing-up liquid, then a rinse under the cold tap.

"All done missus," came a voice from the living room. Masie quickly wiped her hands and went to look. There was the TV man proudly standing next to the new TV with its giant colour picture showing. "Oh great," said Masie, clasping her hands together, "Thank you so much." Then she wrote him a cheque, gave him a £10 tip and he departed.

David Attenborough was on the screen talking about badgers and showing a family of them gambolling about. Masie's favourite! She loved wildlife programmes in general and David Attenborough in particular. She sat down to watch, just for a minute, but minutes have a habit of stretching.

A very loud knocking at the door woke Masie from the doze she'd slipped in to. She jumped up and answered it to Beryl, her new friend from next door who cried: "The Street's all running water and it's all coming out of your back door!"

"Oh my God!" wailed Masie in horror as she rushed to the kitchen. Upon opening the door, she was greeted with a blue haze in the air and three inches of water at the bottom of the step. In her haste to see the new TV, she'd forgotten to turn the tap off then dozed off, leaving the cake to burn. She turned the tap and oven off then opened the back door to admit Beryl. "What am I going to do?" she moaned, "All this is so unexpected, I thought I had it all organised."

"Come on," said Beryl, "No use panicking. We'll soon sort this lot out."

The two women got to work, mopping the floor dry and finishing the washing-up. The charred cake was dumped and the oven cleaned.

"I've just got time to get a cake from the bakers," said a relieved Masie. "I'll ice it myself; Cyril won't know the difference."

"Off you then," said Beryl. "I'll make a cup of tea while you're gone and buy a smoke alarm while you're at it!"

What's in the Name?

Please note: the group and song are real

James – Jimmy to his family, friends and fellow group members had written a song. He'd spent a lot of time over it with many a false start and screwed up balls of paper. His band was called 'The Reapers' and they had a good local following which was nice but they all had their sights set a greater things.

James was sure his song would do it and the others agreed. They also agreed that a new name was needed for the band and James, somewhat rashly, had said: "Leave it to me."

Easier said than done and however hard he tried James couldn't come up with anything that was unusual and different from the usual run of group names. Then fate lent a hand.

His maiden aunt, a very formidable Scottish lady, sent him his usual annual invitation to the Scottish medieval banquet she held every year. The invitation was written as usual on her handmade paper. James sighed.

He had mixed feelings about these banquets. He enjoyed the food and company but found the long journey to Scotland wearisome. But duty is duty and off he went on the Inter City train, spending much of the journey trying to come up with a group name but without success.

He was met at the other end by his aunt Morag in her old Ford. She was wearing, as she always did, her brooch which was fashioned as a large Scottish thistle. Another permanent feature was the Scottish flag she kept flying over her substantial house.

After the usual exchange of pleasantries with his cousins and other relatives, it was time for the banquet. Haggis, solemnly piped in slightly out of tune by an elderly uncle followed by oodles of the sort of food Aunt Morag imagined would have been served at a medieval Caledonian banquet. As it was a very hot day this took place outside under the shade of the trees.

Still thinking of his dilemma between chatting to his cousins, often straining to penetrate their thick accents, James tucked in.

Then he saw a hedgehog slowly walking across the lawn and watched, fascinated, as it sort of clambered over fallen twigs. He knew people kept hedgehogs as pets, even giving them names. This one was obviously wild so didn't have a name. Then James started and nearly choked on a piece of roast wild boar he was eating. He'd got it! The name! He wrote it down as soon as he was able so he wouldn't forget it and couldn't wait to tell the rest of the band.

Back home they all gathered for their usual Wednesday evening practice and James announced the name. All were in enthusiastic agreement. A studio was hired and a demo disc was made which was hawked round several record companies. The lads waited with bated breath.

At last, they got a positive response and the song was released as a single. It went to number one in the charts which turned the band professional.

The song was *It's Good News Week* by Hedgehoppers Anonymous.

A Memory Lapse

"Are you sure you can remember everything?" said Peggy as she got ready to depart.

"Of course," replied Joe, her husband. "I've painted before as you well know."

"Well I'll be off then," she said, giving him a quick peck on the cheek, "see you Monday."

That gave Joe a whole weekend to get the back bedroom painted. Just two colours in water-based emulsion, a piece of cake and with Peggy at her sisters he could do it at his own leisure.

After she'd gone, Joe drove to the large Homebase store on the trading estate and spent a pleasant hour browsing among all their many and varied wares. Like most men he enjoyed looking at tools and thinking of all the things he could do with them. Men's toys, I suppose you could say. At last, he chose the paint, some nice new brushes and several grades of sandpaper. Then home, a quick micro waved pizza, a bit of television then bed.

The next day, a Saturday, Joe spent rubbing down, working from the coarsest to the finest grades of sandpaper until everything was as smooth as it could be. Joe carefully hovered up the dust then went over the skirting board with a damp cloth.

After all his hard work, Joe thought he deserved a night out. *It's Saturday,* he thought, *all the lads will be down the pub,* so off he went.

Well, he did have a good night. The lads were pleased to see him and after many rounds in more than one pub they finished the evening enjoying a rather boisterous curry in an Indian restaurant. Joe eventually tottered home after many a "G'night, gotta do thish again shometime." Once home he fell into – or rather on to – the bed and slept like non-howling infant.

The next morning the world didn't seem so good to Joe. The concrete block he felt he was wearing on his head restricted his movements somewhat and his normal joie de vivre became very muted indeed.

"Gotta get on," he said to himself and he felt rather better after coffee, aspirin and a bacon sandwich. He then set to work painting the room. Quick drying paint so he was able to apply two coats which he did with great care, doing his best to ignore the concrete block which, although somewhat lighter, was still there. At last, the room was done and looked very smart with its new pale blue walls and gleaming dove-grey skirting boards, doors and window frames. Finally satisfied, Joe carefully cleaned his brushes and put them away in the shed together with the unused paint and sandpaper.

Back in the house he sat down and thought. "She'll be pleased with that, all ready for the new carpet coming next week." Then it was another micro waved pizza and an early night.

Monday morning came, as it always does, and Joe awoke early feeling much his old self. He couldn't wait to see how pleased Peggy would be when she saw the room.

At last, she arrived and after a welcoming hug and kiss Joe ushered her into the freshly-painted room, anticipating her pleased reaction. But there was none.

"You idiot!" she cried "Wow, what?" said a very surprised Joe. "I said blue woodwork and grey walls to match the new carpet!" said Peggy reprovingly. "I knew I should have written it down. Well you'll just have to do it again."

So it was back to homebase for poor Joe. More paint and sandpaper plus another two days' work.

Night on the town with the lads? Forget it!

An Awakening

Paddy looked mournfully at the empty whiskey bottle. Jamesons finest was the only way he could cope with the world these days and he'd never let himself run dry before. Childless and with a wife who'd left him two years before he moped around in his little cottage making sporadic and desultory efforts to keep it clean and as for the garden well, best not to mention that.

Behind him was a life of doing very little, drifting from job to job none of which could be regarded as any kind of career. That he and his wife had been able to buy their cottage was mainly due to her efforts. She had put up with his lack of drive and interest in nothing except adding to Jamesons profits for twenty years but one day simply packed her bags and left him to it, leaving a note to say she wasn't coming back.

Paddy's somewhat blurred world fell about his ears. He'd taken Colleen totally for granted and assumed she'd always be there, working at the mill all week then cooking, washing and cleaning for them both. And now she wasn't and life for Paddy suddenly got very hard and bleak indeed, or rather it would have done if Jamesons, as usual, hadn't come to the rescue.

Paddy sighed as he contemplated the walk across the fields to Shamus' little shop in the village for another bottle of Jamesons' elixir. It was early but Shamus would be open by the time he got there. He'd finished the bottle last night and already his head was beginning to clear to face a reality he didn't want to face. A glass or three of Jamesons would soon cure that!

He set off across the fields, keeping close to the public footpath next to the fence. He couldn't remember the last time he'd been out of bed this early, let alone outdoors. It was a beautiful crisp, clear morning with no wind. Paddy suddenly became aware of the sharp, fresh air entering his lungs and experienced something of a renaissance. This was heady, marvellous!

He walked on, looking around him at the mist rising from the fields and the sheep in them. Cresting a low hill he was confronted by a magnificent magnolia tree in full bloom. He stopped and stared, mouth agape. His head was clear now and he suddenly felt a great sadness as the emptiness of his life struck him. Then he lightened. “That tree doesn’t give up,” he said to himself, then: “Why should I?” He stood for a few minutes, indecisive, then: “Blow Shamus, I’m going home.”

He was about to turn when he heard a faint noise. He stopped and listened. There it was again, coming from the direction of something white against the fence some distance away. He went to investigate and found a tiny lamb caught up in some wire which had been used to repair a hole in the fence, and then come loose. Paddy quickly freed the little creature and picked it up, its little bleating tearing at his heartstrings. It felt soft and warm in his arms and once again he marvelled at this thing called life.

He couldn’t tell whether or not the lamb was injured so he went back to where he knew a gate to the farm was and noted a sign on it which said ‘Labour Wanted’. He located the farmer and handed the lamb over. The farmer soon ascertained that the lamb wasn’t hurt and left it to scamper off to find its mother, thanking Paddy for his trouble.

Paddy then asked about the sign and, on an impulse, volunteered himself. “Okay,” said the farmer, who had heard of him. “I’ll give you a go providing you leave the hard stuff at home.”

“Done,” said Paddy, “and my first job will be to fix that hole in the fence.”

So began Paddy’s new life. He worked hard, found he loved doing it and even sorted his cottage and garden out.

As for the empty bottle, he looked at it each evening and said: “Beat you!”

Friends?

Ron and Jed were firm friends and had been from primary school. They went everywhere together and tended to like the same things, supporting the same football team, watching the same films and frequenting McDonalds every Friday after school.

At 14 years of age, neither had yet sampled the delights of female company although both thought about it. Their respective sisters didn't count, of course.

One day as they were coming out of school Jed was eating a banana. On an impulse, and as they were passing a group of girls, he threw the skin down right under Ron's feet. Of course, Ron trod on it and landed on his backside, his books flying everywhere to the great delight of the girls and the great discomfiture of Ron. Jed's laughter didn't help him either. Revenge must be sought, but how? Jed remained on his guard.

Days passed and Jed relaxed, thinking Ron had forgiven him but Ron still blushed if he happened to pass the girls who pointed and giggled at him.

One day the two friends arranged to go camping. Jed had a tent and the weekend looked to be fine. Ron saw his chance!

He went to his mother's sewing box and took a large, new pin. His father made wine so it was an easy matter to snaffle a cork. He then pushed the pin, point uppermost, into the cork and secreted it into one of the pockets in his haversack.

At their chosen site, the boys erected the tent, laid out their sleeping bags and cooking things and got a fire going.

Ron waited until Jed went off to the loo then retrieved the cork and pin. He judged whereabouts Jed's posterior would be when in his sleeping bag then stood the cork on the ground beneath that spot, the pin protruding into the sleeping bag.

The evening passed quite normally, Ron successfully, albeit with great difficulty, keeping a straight face.

The two friends ate their sausages and beans, cooked over the fire, then lazed about until bedtime. When Jed began to yawn, Ron said: "You may as well turn in if you like, I'll see to the fire." That meant scraping up some dirt and dousing it, you can't leave a fire to its own devices at night (or at any other time).

Off went Jed and after a short delay while he got undressed there came a tremendous bellow followed by Jed leaping so fast his head lifted the tent up, pulling its guy ropes out of the ground. After a struggle, he emerged from the collapsed tent, his face a mask of fury. But Ron was already a dot on the horizon.

A Wrong (Right)?

Nurse Rogers was lost. Map reading never was one of her strong points and now it had let her down completely. It was misty too.

Nurse Rogers was a midwife and had been for the last twenty-six years. She'd lost count of how many babies she'd delivered in that time and now she was trying to get to yet another one.

At 54, she had grown tired of the hustle and bustle of city life around the hospital where she had worked. Not the job, she loved that, it was the dense traffic that had stopped her getting anywhere quickly. This had made her too late on three occasions. The first baby had been delivered by a policeman, the second by the mother's sister and the third one by the father. That last one was the last straw and when she saw a position advertised in the countryside near the sea she took it.

After the hassle of moving, she settled in nicely. Never having married, she was well used to organising herself and was off to her first call which had come in half an hour or so earlier.

Now, in 1975 and well before the advent of satnavs, her old but good Morris Minor nosed its way along a gravelly track which appeared to be heading straight for the sea. "At last, the mist is clearing," she said to herself, "but this can't be right." She determined to go back to the village she had passed through a couple of miles back even though time was of the essence. She didn't want to be late on her first job but it couldn't be helped. Maybe it was a false alarm? They sometimes were.

At last, she found somewhere to turn round but as she did so she noticed something on the grass which looked out of place.

She got out to see what it was, the cool sea breeze ruffling her hair. And saw it was a small picnic hamper. *Odd,* she thought, then above the noise of the wheeling sea birds she heard a faint cry for help although no one could be seen. She shouted: "Hello! Where are you?"

"Over here!" came the reply.

She walked towards the sound and a dozen steps found her standing on the edge of a hole in the ground. It was about ten feet deep and in it was an elderly man with a pair of binoculars slung around his neck. "Are you hurt?" she asked.

"No," he said, "but I can't get out. My stupid fault for coming up here in the mist, I knew the sink hole was there."

What to do? Then nurse Rogers had a brainwave. "Hang on," she said then went to her car and carefully backed it on to the grass. She got her tow rope out of the boot, tied one end to the rear bumper and dropped the other end down to the man, saying: "I'm going to pull you out. I'll drive very slowly."

Back in her car she did drive very slowly enabling the man to 'walk' up the side of the hole while holding on to the rope.

Once out, he thanked nurse Rodgers profusely. "I often come up here to watch the birds," he said. "My wife isn't interested and I enjoy the walk from the village. I thought the mist would have cleared by the time I got here."

Tow rope safely stowed away, together with his picnic basket, she told him where she was supposed to be. "Oh, that's not far," he said, "I'll show you."

Off they went and to her joy nurse Rogers found she wasn't too late. The original call was a false alarm but it wasn't now and a healthy little boy soon made his debut into the world.

On their way back to his village, the man told her his name was Jeff Hodges and it turned out he worked for the Ordnance Survey before retirement. On hearing of her difficulty, he offered to teach her how to read a map properly and after a few visits to his and Mrs Hodges' cottage in the village Nurse Rogers never got lost again!

Revenge

Robert was very attached to an antique painting that hung in his hall. It had been painted by his great, great grandfather and depicted a Victorian dragoon on a horse.

Robert had never married and eked out a living via his old age pension and the rent from a lodger. His previous lodger having departed for pastures new Robert advertised for a replacement and soon had another in the person of James Wright, a very surly and gruff elderly man whom Robert hoped would keep himself to himself.

When James caught sight of the painting, he snorted and said: “Who painted that rubbish?”

“My great, great grandfather,” replied Robert, wishing he hadn’t already taken Mr Wright’s money.

“Huh,” sneered James, “a waste of a good frame if you ask me.” He then stomped off to his room and Robert noticed he had a limp and further noticed the round stump of a wooded peg leg beneath his left trouser leg.

Over the succeeding days James made a critical comment almost every time he passed the painting. “Do I have to see that thing? Why don’t you burn it?” were just two of the many remarks he made.

Robert became angrier and angrier and sought revenge.

James was in the habit of taking an afternoon nap and Robert wondered if he removed his wooden leg at those times. The next afternoon he crept into James’ room after assuring himself of James’ snores and, sure enough, there was the leg resting on a chair. Robert gently removed it then took it down to his shed, which he rarely visited these days. He got his old, rusty tenon saw down from its nail and sawed part way through the wooden leg. He hoped he had judged it right; he didn’t want Mr Wright to discover the crime whilst on his premises. He then quietly replaced the leg.

That day was the end of the week and when James came to pay his weekly rent Robert said: "I'm sorry, but I don't want that. I want you to leave because I'm fed up with your insults regarding my great, great grandfather's painting."

With a lot of huffing and puffing, James went and got his belongings and left, after saying: "At least I won't have to look at that thing again."

So Robert didn't witness the downfall of James which didn't occur until some days later. He wasn't badly hurt and found the saw cut in his leg. His problem was that he'd upset so many people in the past that, although he suspected Robert, he knew he'd never prove it.

His replacement leg was a metal one!

A Friendly Line

George trudged through the ancient forest, another lonely afternoon and evening looming ahead.

He had been to the village to do his weekly shop and was now returning to his lonely little cottage at the edge of the forest. George and his wife had enjoyed the peace, stillness and solitude and they had together explored all the many paths through the trees and bushes, learning the habits of squirrels, rabbits, badgers as well as the occasional fox or deer. Birds were special favourites and they each carried a small pair of binoculars every time they went wandering.

George's Helen had died 18 months previously, leaving him alone. Their grown-up children and grandchildren came to visit and those times were happy ones but the long gaps in between seemed interminable. George and Helen had never mixed with the villagers, preferring their own company and George now wished they had been more outgoing.

Suddenly his eyes, which had lost none of their sharpness due to age, spotted some fishing line draped over a bush. The river was some distance away from the path and villagers did fish in it sometimes. "Careless idiot," muttered George to himself, "an animal could get tangled up in that."

He began to wind the line round his free hand and could see it stretching away into the distance. He sighed but determined to retrieve it all. The morning was fresh and bright and George certainly didn't mind an excuse for a walk.

Eventually, now with a large ball of line round his hand, he could see the river sparkling ahead, his path to it had been very meandering.

Another fifty feet found him at the river and the end of the line which was attached to a fly fishing rod. Next to it sat a man on a little foldaway seat fly fishing with a similar rod.

"Any luck?" asked George.

"No," replied the man, "but I haven't been here long."

George held up the ball of line and said: "This must be yours then."

“Yes,” said the man. “I’ve just moved in to the village and I was told about this river. Also that it could be difficult to find, so I left a trail of line back to the path so I could find my way back again. I would have reeled it in as I went back.”

George introduced himself and pointed out that he was very familiar with the forest and all its byways. The man was called Reg and he told George he was also a widower and had sold his large town house, preferring a quiet village existence.

Thus began a firm friendship. Reg had family too and both families met up occasionally at George’s cottage for a barbecue, the grandchildren shrieking with delight as they chased each other among the trees or went very quiet when they spotted a rabbit or squirrel.

No more lonely evenings for George or Reg. George was ex-army and Reg ex-navy so much good natured banter there!

If you ever see fishing line lying about pick it up (beware of hooks). You will be helping the environment and you never know who or what you might find at the end of it!

A TT Winner

The TT motor-cycle races, held each year on the Isle of Man, always attract huge crowds of people, both motor-cyclists and otherwise. Hotels and boarding houses are fully booked some weeks before the races are due to start so latecomers, of which there are many, have to bring tents or just rough it. Trying to get a place near the start or finish lines was a hopeless task for most people.

Jim and Wally had attended each year for the past five years but, fed up with the overcrowding, hit on the idea of watching the races from a hot air balloon.

Accordingly, one was hired complete with pilot, leaving Jim and Wally praying for good weather. They were in luck, the whole week was sunny and warm with hardly a breath of wind and the two friends plus the pilot had an unencumbered view of all the races.

In the evenings, they stayed in a hotel which was well away from the public roads used for the races and thus didn't charge extortionate prices. They could thus keep away from the largest of the crowds and browse around the shops. It was one of these forays during the evening before the last race that Wally decided to buy himself a new pair of Dr Marten's boots.

The last day dawned, fine and hot like all the others, and the two aeronauts were well placed to see the last race, the Senior TT with unlimited engine capacity and the climax of the week.

The end approached and with three miles to go a gaggle of six riders jostled for first place. Wally found his new boots too hot so he took them off and, without thinking, placed them on the rim of the basket. A sudden lurch, although slight, was, to Wally's horror, enough to send his boots into space.

Down on the road Bill Hunt was lying seventh. He had no chance of winning and didn't expect to, He'd done well to get this far as this was his first Senior.

Suddenly he saw the gaggle of riders ahead of him break up in total disarray. Brake lights glowed and bikes swerved this way and that to avoid each other. Before they had a chance to recover, Bill swept pass them and to his great joy went on to win. He had seen the problem; some idiot had left a pair of boots on the road.

After landing, Wally didn't wait to see the champion's ceremony. He sneaked back to the hotel, put his old shoes on and stayed there until it was time to go home. Jim couldn't stop laughing but never gave him away. Well, what are friends for? The pilot kept shtum too; he didn't want his balloon blamed.

Money Bags and Bags of It!

I believe it is still the case that pre-decimal and obsolete coins and banknotes can still be exchanged for their face value but there are, as you might expect, a couple of snags.

I understand that the amount tendered must be substantial (whatever 'substantial' means) and they can only be exchanged at the Bank of England which is hard luck if you don't live anywhere near it.

Apparently, this doesn't appear to be the case in Germany, where branches of their banks will exchange deutschmarks for Euros and it is estimated that some 12.65 billion deutschmarks are still in circulation.

Our own powers that be know most people here will either have too few coins to be worth bothering about or wouldn't be prepared to pay the high postage costs involved in sending a large and heavy number of coins to the Bank of England. The collective value of these coins must be great but the government, which has derived tax from it almost every time it changed hands, will never have to redeem its value.

Of course, some coins will be worth much more than their face value. A £1 gold sovereign has a scrap value of over 200 times that, even if very worn and with no collector value. The same applies to silver. Up to 1920 our silver coins were of sterling silver which is 92.5% pure. To help pay for items we had bought from the Americans during World War I this was then reduced to 50% or half-silver. The same thing happened after World War II when all silver was removed after 1946 except for Maundy money and special collector's issues. Back in the 1970s I heard of a taxi driver who scrapped £600 worth of silver coins when he could get 14 times for pre '20 silver and 6 times for pre '47. A nice little earner!

Back in Germany the manager, Heiko Ennen, of the Oldenburg branch of the Bundesbank must have been very surprised when a truck full of coins turned up. They were brought by a couple from Bremervorde who said their father had collected them over a thirty year period. They were one and two pfennig coins, weighed 2.5 tons and were contained in freezer bags. Herr Ennen confirmed that they would exchange such coins without fees, something our own banking system might care to consider.

An employee, Wolfgang Kemerit, volunteered to count them, no doubt to the great relief of his colleagues, and spent six months in doing so in his spare time. Many were corroded together and could not be put through a counting machine so he counted all 1.2 million of them individually, value about 8,000 Euros. There were also about three kilos of foreign coins.

Herr Kemerit said: “I like to do this kind of thing, so it was no problem.”

Maybe he needs to get out more!

Bobby and the Cow

Bobby loved his cow. Well, it wasn't really his cow because at nine years old he was too young to own one. Buttercup was one of a herd owned by his father who grazed them on the lush, emerald green grass which covered the fields where they lived.

Bobby didn't know why he loved Buttercup over all the other cows but it may well have been because she came up to him one day, gazed at him with large, sorrowful eyes and lowed softly. Perhaps she fell in love with him, assuming cows can feel love of course.

Bobby always looked for her in the morning before he went to school when she would walk up to him and allow him to stroke and pat her huge flanks. At home time, she'd be there waiting for him, head over the five-barred gate and tail gently switching from side to side.

At week-ends, it would be Bobby who led Buttercup, followed by the rest of the herd, into the milking shed where his mother, father and big sister Elsie were there to hook the cows up to the milking machines. All except Buttercup of course, that was Bobby's job.

Bobby would often tell Buttercup he loved her and she would softly moo. Perhaps she understood, who knows a cow's mind?

One awful day, forever etched in Bobby's memory, Buttercup became ill. Her mooing became mournful and the sad look in her eyes came near to breaking his heart. He begged his father to do something, especially when he overheard him saying to his mother: "Aye, she's offn her food too 'n her milk's no good what with blood in it 'n all." Bobby knew his parents hoped Buttercup would get better on her own, cows did that sometimes.

"Have to be the vet then," said his mother reluctantly as vets were an expense they could ill afford. "I hope it won't be the other 'cos that'd break Bobby's heart."

A chill ran up Bobby's spine and he went cold. He didn't quite know what 'the other' was but he sensed it was something awful and final. The vet was called and would come the next day. No sleep for Bobby that night.

The next day being Saturday meant no school for Bobby who went out early to tell Buttercup that a man was coming to make her better. It was a lovely morning with the dew sparkling like diamonds on the grass but Bobby was too worried about his beloved Buttercup to notice things like that. She looked thin and dejected, bringing him near to tears.

The vet arrived, a lady rather than the man Bobby had assumed and, after examining Buttercup, she said: "She's swallowed something which she can't pass. I can't tell where it is so it will mean a big operation to find it. I have to tell you that she might not survive." Again Bobby went cold. Then he remembered something.

One of the fields lay over an old dump, the ashes it contained helping to make the grass as lush as it was. Ploughing sometimes brought odd bits of junk to the surface, the odd bottle or piece of rusty metal. He ran into the house and grabbed the Argos catalogue, something he loved browsing through, quickly found the page he was looking for and ran back to where the vet and his family were standing round disconsolately with his beloved Buttercup.

"She might have swallowed metal," he panted. His finger pointed to a metal detector, "One of these might find it."

"Worth a try," said the vet. "My son's got one, I'll go and get him."

She left and returned a short while later accompanied with a strapping teenager carrying a metal detector who blushed when Elsie smiled at him.

The offending object was soon located. Just a small operation was required and that produced an old brass door knob.

Buttercup soon recovered and Bobby kept the door knob on his bedside table, polishing it until it shone like new to remind him of the day he nearly lost the love of his life.

Bikers Unite

Brett rode his motor-bike gingerly along the main street of the unfamiliar village. He didn't like riding on cobbles. Then a sign caught his eye – a café! A cup of tea would be most welcome after his Sunday morning ride out on this chilly early spring day.

Inside a warming cuppa followed by another one and a nice doughnut went down a treat. Refreshed and warmed he returned to his bike to find an old man looking at it while he leant on a walking-stick.

"Your bike?"

"Yes mate."

"Japanese, I suppose?"

"Yeah, it's a Yamaha Virago, 1100 cc V-twin. Some call it a poor man's Harley but I like it and it's reliable. You a biker then?"

"I was," said the old man. "In the army like. I was a Don R – despatch rider to you – but a wound put paid to all that."

"Why, what happened?" asked Brett, sensing that the old man wanted to tell him.

"It was in France a week after D-Day," came the prompt reply. "Me and my 'oppo was ordered to H.Q. on our bikes. We wuz goin' through some woods when a jerry popped up and got me in the leg. Smashed me knee so's I can't straighten me left leg and that was the end of the army and bikin' for me. My 'oppo got the Jerry though, potted the blighter with one shot. 'Ere, I've got a photo." And so saying he pulled out a wallet and extracted a photograph from it which he handed to Brett saying: "That's me, just before D-Day."

The picture showed a grinning young man standing behind a single-cylinder motor-cycle.

"Lovely she was," went on the old man, "I used to love riding her. A real old thumper."

"What's the white star on the tank for?" asked Brett.

“All vehicles involved in D-Day ’ad ‘em,” came the reply, “same as all the planes ’ad black and white stripes.” For some reason, Brett mentally noted the bike’s registration number, WD 6248. The old man went on:

“I kept me uniform though. The big shed where we got our demob suits was bedlam, so once I got me suit I lifted me uniform and scarpered. It still fits and I wears it every Remembrance Sunday at the memorial. You see the church tower over there? Well it’s next to that.”

After a bit more chat and a handshake, Brett took his leave.

A few weeks later Brett was at a bike auto-jumble. All sorts of bike bits were on sale covering bikes from all eras including complete bikes in various states of preservation. Brett liked wandering around, chatting and admiring others’ bikes.

Then a bright red one next to a stall caught his eye. It was on a low trailer which was hitched to a 4X4. An old BSA single. Brett moved closer then stopped dead, his mouth agape. WD 6248. It was the old man’s bike!

The stallholder was also elderly. Brett approached him. “What’s the story on that then?” he enquired, nodding at the bike.

“My dad bought it as army surplus,” replied the stallholder. “He eventually passed it on to my son who painted it that ghastly colour. But now he’s into cars and wants me to sell it for him. It still runs OK.”

An idea began to form in Brett’s mind and his query: “How much?” was followed by the inevitable haggling. Finally a deal was struck and the next weekend the bike was delivered to Brett’s home where the cash changed hands.

In the meantime, Brett had told his family of his plan and his father, mother and sister all wanted to be involved. The internet provided all they needed, the right colour paint, cables, tyres etc. While they waited for it all to arrive, the bike was stripped, its engine, gearbox and dynamo de-greased and cleaned, the frame, tank and mudguards rubbed down, the brakes overhauled and the lights checked. Fresh engine and gearbox oil was the last item.

Then the paint and parts came and the bike slowly resumed its original guise. The old webbing panniers were blancoed and the brass buckles polished. Finally a star was drawn on paper, cut out and used as a stencil for the tank, white of course.

The next Remembrance Sunday Brett rode the bike to the village memorial while his family followed in their car. They were early and hid themselves and the bike round a corner. People started to arrive and soon the old man appeared in his uniform, cap badge, medals and boot toe caps all gleaming. He caught sight of Brett.

"'Allo, young 'un. What you doin' 'ere?"

"Got a surprise for you," said a smiling Brett, then he shouted: "Dad!" His father appeared wheeling the bike. The old man stared in amazement and clapped his hand to his head. "She's my old bike!" he finally managed to say in a choking voice. "Where did you find her?"

So Brett told him. The old man couldn't mount the bike so he sat on it side saddle and once again held the handlebars and moved the choke and advance/retard levers back and forth as the memories came flooding back. "Well I'll be blowed," he kept saying, then: "see that dent in the tank? That's where she fell over when I got shot."

A local reporter and photographer were on hand, as they were every year, and a photo of the old man standing once again behind his old bike with a big grin on his face appeared in the local paper together with his story.

From that day on, Brett would ride the bike to the old man's house at least once each month where he would enjoy his wife's home-made cakes and listen enthralled to the old man's war stories.

He still hated the cobbles though!

A Cold Cure

Albert Close was a cul-de-sac which meant no through road to traffic but free passage for pedestrians to the one-way street which ran along its end. It split into two at the junction with an oblong of grass in between which the council kept tidy.

One very snowy winter the local children built two snowmen on the oblong in the form of a hold-up. One had a flat cap, a mask and an old hair drier as a gun. The other one was in a hands-up posture with twigs for hands and a trilby hat. Both had carrots for noses and faced each other on the grass oblong. Other children walking to school admired the two snowmen as they threw snowballs at one another.

But then the Smith brothers appeared on the scene and the other children hurried away. The Smiths were two in number and notorious bullies. Appeals to their parents were ignored. When they spotted the snowmen, they grinned at each other and, as one, ran up to them and kicked them to pieces to the dismay of other children passing by. Some were accompanied by their mothers but their admonishments had no effect on the Smiths.

The Harrisses lived in Albert Close and Mrs Harris viewed the wreck of the snowmen after her two boys told her what had happened. She told her husband about it when he came home from work.

Mr Harris waited until their boys were in bed then told his wife how they could teach the bullies a lesson. "We'll need to work fast," he said.

Mr Harris had noticed a stack of bricks behind their shed left there by a previous tenant. When all was dark and quiet, Mr and Mrs Harris rebuilt the snowmen, but this time each one had a pile of bricks concealed inside it.

The next morning the children on their way to school once again marvelled at the two snowmen and, of course, the Smith brothers appeared too. Once again they grinned as they rushed full tilt at the snowmen and each gave one a good, hard kick. Their resultant howls brought people out of their houses but the ruined snowmen and the bricks told their own story.

I've never suffered from broken toes myself but to judge by the noise made by the Smiths the pain must have been considerable and yet more as they limped and hopped back home.

Then it was a trip to the hospital the removal of a shoe and sock from one foot each, x-rays, plaster of Paris and bandages all rendering life rather inconvenient for some weeks to come.

The police were called but the Harrisses' footprints were mixed up with many others and, being aware of the Smith's reputation, they didn't enquire too closely.

I don't know if there is a word to describe a fear of snowmen but, if there is, the Smith brothers suffered from it for some time to come.

Smuggler's Arrest

It was Tom Sharpe's first day with His Majesty's Revenue and Customs Authority and he was being briefed by the team leader Mike Smith who pointed to a large-scale map on the wall.

"As you can see," he began. "We are less than two miles from the border and the river ends in a delta which splits into nine separate streams into the sea and we have to patrol them all. The smugglers always seem to know where we are which makes it easy for them to avoid us."

"What are they smuggling?" asked Tom.

"Oh, the usual as far as we can tell," came the reply, "cigarettes, spirits, possibly drugs. Stuff that's portable and easily disposed of. We don't hear their boat so we assume it has an electric motor as it's too far to row."

"Hmm," mused Tom. "What about when they go back empty?"

"They don't," said Mike. "We think they rendezvous down the main river, remove the cargo, lift the boat out of the water and take it back over the border by road with a legitimate excuse for doing so. We need to catch them in the act."

"Someone must be tipping them off," said Tom with a frown, "Lights? Radio?"

"Nope," replied Mike with a shake of the head, "we've watched for lights and our radio scanner has never picked up anything."

And so the puzzle remained. For the next week, Tom rode on the patrol boat as it cruised up and down one or other of the nine streams that formed the river delta. An area devoid of buildings apart from an old windmill which was some distance from the river.

"I know those guys are here somewhere," said Mike grimly. "I can feel it." But the still of the night remained unbroken apart from the sound of their own engine.

The next day Tom noticed something. "Tell me about that windmill," he said to Steve, one of his colleagues.

“It’s derelict,” said Steve. “The workings were removed years ago and it’s just a shell now plus the sails of course. No one’s been in there for years.”

“That’s it!” exclaimed Tom, banging his fist on the desk, “I thought I saw the sails move slightly. They’re using them as a signal!”

Mike was told and they went to the mill.

“That padlock looks pretty new to me,” remarked Steve on viewing it.

So a trap was laid. When a man came at night and opened the lock, he was nabbed. In his pocket was a paper showing nine subtle sail movements, one for each delta stream. The smugglers took turns to operate it and they had a very good view over the area from the top of the mill. Those on the boat used binoculars to view the sails, nicely outlined against the lights of the distant town.

So the sails were set to indicate the customs boat being way upstream in one of the other streams whereas it waited in stream one. And that was the end of that particular gang of smugglers!

An Odyssey

We walked on the sand in the gloom. It would maybe an adventure. Then we saw a lady's shoe in the sand. What was that doing there? We looked around. Here was a man's hat, there a glove with a pair of spectacles. We could see other things as far as we could see, which wasn't very far.

Puzzled, we walked on then a wall appeared out of the gloom. A cliff? No, it was iron that seemed to be melting. The side of a great ship! We put our ears to it. Nothing but silence inside, dead silence.

We found a way in and were confronted by a magnificent staircase down which one could make a grand entrance. An equally grand lady, her silk gown rustling and her many jewels flashing in the soft glow of the chandeliers would slowly descend, one hand on the banister and the other linked to her husband's arm nodding condescendingly to any who acknowledged her until she joined the rich gathering below.

But not today. Just debris on the stairs and one banister, broken, leaning out drunkenly. The room was empty and the chandeliers long extinguished.

Silence.

We move into the richly-appointed dining room. A hum of expectancy as the first waiters appear with steaming tureens? No. Broken tables and chairs thrown everywhere and more of them in a heap against the wall. Crockery, cutlery and broken wine glasses abound, the snow-white linen having rotted long ago.

Silence.

We pass into the kitchen where another scene of mayhem greets us. No cooks banging and bustling about. An overturned cooker, another huge heap of cutlery and broken crockery and pots and pans thrown about.

Silence.

We move into the men's smoking room where the rich enjoyed their expensive cigars, brandy and port. Wingate, the oil king, with one elbow on the mantel-shelf and one foot on the fender. But he is not here today and neither is anyone else. Just:

Silence.

Next door is the lady's drawing room where the wives of the rich sip their tiny glasses of sherry and discuss the latest Paris fashions, but they are gone today and only the shards of broken mirrors remain.

Silence.

We go forwards into another large room, not as opulent as those we have just left but impressive nonetheless. A big crowd laughing, chattering, eating, drinking or dancing to the small band? No, just more broken chairs and tables, the remains of a bass drum in one corner and a battered trumpet in another. The bulging ceiling seems in danger of imminent collapse.

Silence.

Curiously, we make our way to the engine room where these huge monoliths send their pulsing, throbbing throughout the ship. Usually deafening this close but not today. Now they stand like stricken giants, never to move again.

Silence.

The boiler room, usually a cacophony of shovelling coal and roaring, white-hot furnaces is anything but today. Coal and shovels are strewn about and the furnaces are black and dead. No life.

Silence.

Lastly, we look into the cabins and see bed linen and clothes of both sexes all twisted together in inextricable tangles here, there and everywhere. Overturned wardrobes. Half empty cosmetic bottles hover before our eyes.

Silence.

We creep away. So where are the 2,200 souls supposed to be aboard? What has caused such catastrophic devastation? Of course it was the sea.

So we leave the great ship down there in her deep, cold, pitch-black, utterly silent, watery grave.

Hairbrained

"We have a spy in our midst," said a grim-faced Mr Jeffries from behind his paper-laden desk.

"Are you sure?" replied Peter Jones, his deputy. It was the beginning of Autumn 1940 with what Churchill had dubbed 'The Battle of Britain' at its height and in which the Luftwaffe were trying and failing to destroy the Royal Air Force in the air and on the ground. Our factories were targets too and to combat that a series of shadow factories were set up, well away from the larger towns but close to smaller ones so that labour, much of it female, could be recruited.

A team of agents scoured the countryside for suitable sites and, having found them, reported back to Mr Jeffries and his team. Each agent had his own area independent of the others.

Upon receipt of a promising site, Mr Jeffries and his team swung into action to arrange things. They would locate and contact the land owner and arrange for the building to be delivered, an easily erected edifice of angle iron and corrugated iron sheets, very hot in summer and cold in winter. From the air, they looked like warehouses although they were painted in camouflage colours. The Ministry of Supply would be alerted who would decide what machinery was needed, arrange for it to be delivered and installed and local labour to be recruited and trained. But too many of these factories were being bombed, often before they've even started production.

"We lost four factories last month," went on Mr Jeffries, "which is too many to be a coincidence. Someone is pinpointing them for the Germans."

Peter Jones sighed. The twenty-strong team had all been thoroughly vetted which meant that a spy would be very difficult to find, especially if he or she was a 'sleeper'. Sleepers were spies who were infiltrated into another country where they laid low, sometimes for years, until they were activated by their handler and in the meantime obtaining jobs in places where they could be useful. A handler often controlled several spies and were the conduit through which information was channelled and via which the spies were paid and received instructions.

"The last one was making propellers for our aircraft," said Mr Jeffries gloomily, "Not to mention the 23 killed and 18 injured. I'm afraid I'm going to have to put this one on you Peter. Do what you can but don't make it too obvious or our spy will go to ground. We have to catch him or her."

"I'll do my best, sir," said Jones, well aware of the gravity of the situation as he left the office. But where to start? Workers were allowed to take home work of a non-sensitive nature but their briefcases were always thoroughly searched.

A few days later, with nothing to report to Mr Jeffries, Jones was washing his hands in the gent's toilet when another man came in. Jones recognised him as a Dutchman, Jan Van Rintj, a newish member of the team. It was a very hot day as the whole summer had been, probably the end of a very warm period which had begun in the Middles Ages. Ideal for aerial activity and became known later as 'Spitfire Summer'.

Jones and van Rintj passed the time of day and Jones grinned as the other man removed a toupee and mopped his face and a large bald spot with a large handkerchief. "You could leave it off in this weather," he said jokingly.

"Oh no," replied Van Rintj in perfect English. "I've had it nearly 20 years now; I'd feel naked without it." He replaced it, used the urinal, washed his hands and the two men left together, Jones trying hard to conceal a frown.

He went straight to Mr Jeffries office. "Van Rintj's your man," he said.

"Are you sure?" came the reply. "He came over after the Germans invaded Holland last May."

Jones was sure and a thorough search of Van Rintj's flat was carried out while he was at work. Concealed behind a wardrobe was found a large scale Ordnance Survey map with shadow factory locations marked on it plus papers showing Van Rintj was a member of the Dutch Nazi Party. Other papers enabled his handler and other spies to be apprehended.

Upon confrontation, Van Rintj confessed. When a site was found, he marked it on his map then phoned its precise location to his handler. High flying German reconnaissance aircraft would then watch the site and photograph it when a building appeared. The Luftwaffe would then bomb it.

"Well done, Peter," said Mr Jeffries, shaking his hand. "But how did you get on to him?"

"He wears a toupee," replied Jones, "and I saw him take it off and put it on. I was a barber before the war and he claimed to have been wearing it for nearly 20 years. I knew he was lying because he put it on back to front!"

A Neat Catch

The Plumbs lived in a nice three storey house in a better part of town. Professor Plumb taught English at the local university while his wife had given up a promising academic career to bring up their twin sons. The boys, like their father, were big, strapping, lads aged seventeen and both attended college where they played in its rugby team.

The family all loved crossword puzzles in which the professor, as one would expect, was especially proficient.

One afternoon the twins and their mother were struggling to complete the last clue in one which was 'A foreign entanglement' with a nine letter answer. They spent some time to no avail until Mrs Plumb came up with 'imbroglio'. They thought that was it but no, it didn't fit with the other letters they had. When the professor came in, he took one look, picked up the pen and wrote in 'spaghetti'.

One winter a cat burglar appeared in the area. His modus operandi was as follows:

He never cased the joint, as the saying goes, in the day time as a lone stranger strolling about would arouse suspicion. But on a cold, wet, windy night he would sally forth clad in black from head to toe at a time when it was pitch dark but still too early for bedtime. He found it easy to hide from the odd car or pedestrian he did see.

He looked for drainpipes running close to bedroom windows which were rarely locked even though ground floor ones were. Closed curtains indicated a sleeping occupant, perhaps a child, so he ignored those. As for others he quickly shinned up the drainpipe, slipped the window catch and silently ransacked the room for jewellery, watches and money which he would stow in a pouch on his belt.

The police were foxed, they could never be in the right place at the right time and a neighbourhood watch scheme didn't work because no one wanted to be out patrolling in such bad weather.

Professor Plumb put his mind to the problem with the result that workmen appeared one day with a length of drainpipe made of lead.

They removed the top section of the Plumbs drainpipe which passed close to a top floor window and replaced it with the lead one, pinning it only loosely to the wall and painting it to match the rest of the pipe. A wire was soldered to it and led through the window, which was slightly ajar, to a switch which was connected to another wire which led to a strobe light down in the living room. Pull the wire, the switch would be thrown and the strobe would flash.

A few weeks of good weather passed then it abruptly changed to freezing rain and strong winds. Burglar weather! Each night the Plumbs waited in the living room watching television.

Two other houses were burgled before the thief came across the Plumbs' but at last he did. The tell-tale wire wasn't visible from the ground although he saw to his delight that the window wasn't quite closed.

Up the pipe he went in his fast, athletic way. No problem until he got to the topmost section, when he was dismayed to find himself moving away from the wall. The pipe was bending! Already he was too far away from the wall to reach the pipe still fixed to it and he was too high to jump.

Of course the wire snapped but not before it had thrown the switch. Downstairs in the living room the strobe began flashing. Instantly, Mrs Plumb phoned the police while the three men donned anoraks and rushed outside. There they found the burglar hanging from the now near-horizontal pipe and working his way hand over hand to the wall. He reached it and quickly shinned down the pipe into the arms of three burly males.

The police duly arrived and led the miscreant away in handcuffs after gazing in some wonderment at the horizontal pipe.

The next day, the weather having improved somewhat, the workmen returned to restore the drainpipe to its normal configuration. A policeman came too, to take statements from the Plumbs. He laughed when he heard how the burglar had been caught and asked: "How did you think of that?"

"Our name," replied Professor Plumb. "The Latin name for lead is plumbum!"

In from the Cold

Within the Turner family, Phillip was a bit of an outcast. Not that they were snobs particularly even though they regarded themselves as connoisseurs of music, wine and the arts. Except for Phillip, who hated wine, drank Guinness, listened to ABBA and either liked or disliked any picture he saw. His parents, two sisters and one brother all worked in their own business from which they all derived a pretty good income, Turner's ice cream being a very popular consumable. But not Phillip.

No way would Phillip work indoors and to him board meetings and paper work were the stuff of nightmares. He loved his job as a refuse collector as it was outdoors, kept him fit and, most important of all, enabled him to keep an eye out for anything fit for 'reusing' as he called it. Even as a child his sisters called him 'Scallyrag' and his mother often had to clear away the broken toys he'd found on the local dump and tried unsuccessfully to mend.

As an adult, he would poke around in any skips he saw and every Sunday morning he could be found rooting around on the local dump, something that wouldn't normally be allowed but as he worked for the council he got away with it.

Phillip rented a small ground floor flat which he'd furnished with items he'd found, all repaired in a somewhat slipshod manner as his DIY skills were not great. His telephone was a novelty one in the form of Donald Duck which he'd found in working order and which 'quacked' when anyone called which wasn't too often as his family took a 'he's not with us' attitude to him. His washing machine and television had to be bought as he wasn't up to repairing such items.

One Sunday morning Phillip was out on the dump as usual when he found a painting rolled up inside a cardboard tube. He unrolled it to find a rather nice landscape even though the paint was flaking off in one or two places which was probably why it had been thrown away. He took it home and over the ensuing week or so made a fairly decent frame for it, hanging it on the wall next to the door.

Phillip wasn't actually abandoned by his family. He always joined them for Christmas, birthdays and weddings etc. even though his mode of dress was considered 'working class' by his trying-not-to-be-snobs family and one or another of them popped in to see him occasionally. And so it was that one Saturday his brother, Henry, called carrying a welcome six-pack of Guinness.

"Hi Phil," he said, "You okay?"

"Yes, fine thanks," came the reply as Phillip took the six-pack, opened a can and took a long swig. "Thanks for this. How's the family?"

"Oh fine," replied Henry, "but we've got a problem with the business. Demand has grown so much that we're having a job supplying everybody and three of our regulars are threatening to go elsewhere. We need to expand."

"Sorry to hear that," said Phillip, wiping his lips with the back of his hand. "Can't you get a bank loan?"

"Yes," said Henry, "but Mum and Dad aren't keen on that at their age and interest would have to be paid. Our business is largely seasonal as you know. But that seems to be the only option."

After more inconsequential chat, Henry turned to go and noticed the painting. "That's nice," he said, "very amateur, of course."

"I like it," rejoined Phillip, "makes me feel outdoors when I'm not."

Henry noticed a two-inch patch where the paint had flaked off and looked closer. He gave a start. "Have you got a magnifying glass?" he asked.

After a rummage in a drawer, Phillip produced one and Henry stared through it at the patch. Finally he said: "There's another painting under here, this should be x-rayed."

"Why?" asked Phillip, "is it ill?"

"No," laughed Henry, "but you might have something special here."

So Henry took the picture and paid for it to be x-rayed. A ghostly picture emerged of people in a busy street and that magic signature: L.S. Lowry. The top painting was professionally removed and the Lowry pronounced genuine, fetching many thousands of pounds at auction.

Phillip was dumbfounded. "All that money!" he exclaimed. "Henry please use it to expand the business."

"I was hoping you'd say that," said Henry, blushing. "We'll make you a partner."

“No thanks, not for me,” came the reply.

“You’d be a sleeping partner.”

“What’s that then?”

“You don’t actually do anything,” Henry explained, “but you get an income for your investment providing we make a profit – which we will, believe me.”

And that’s how it was. Everybody was happy and Phillip wasn’t so much of an outcast any more.

Nearly Lost

Ragnald liked his new country which would someday be called England. It was a lot warmer than his old one which we now know as Scandinavia. More rain, of course, but the lush grass and forests teeming with wildlife more than made up for that. He'd come over with his parents and his two younger sisters as settlers rather than invaders. That part had been done by his ancestors and there was nothing he liked better than listening to the tales from those times in the evening by the fire and how a warrior could get to Valhalla only by dying with a sword in his hand.

He had a sword. It was an old one of his father's given to him on his tenth birthday. It had been rusty with disuse but he cleaned it by thrusting it in and out of sand then smearing it with pig fat to protect it and making it easier to draw from its scabbard. He would get a new one on his sixteenth birthday but in the meantime he was very proud of the one he had even though at eleven years of age he had to hold it with both hands. The sea wasn't far away and Ragnald spent lots of time there walking along a deserted part he'd found listening to the wind and waves talking to him and swinging his sword about to strengthen up his sword arm as his grandfather had told him.

To get to this part of the beach a marsh had to be crossed which is why no one else bothered with it. That suited Ragnald, he preferred the solitude. Despite warnings from his parents, he'd found a way across after many false starts and a way, once found, he'd marked with wooden stakes cut with his sword and stuck in the ground at intervals. The marshy parts looked black and ominous, some covered with a green algae. He'd pushed his sword into it at several places but couldn't feel the bottom. Don't want to fall in there!

One day he had just reached the beginning of the marsh when he heard a movement in the bushes which grew there. Drawing his sword he went to investigate and found a fox snared in a rabbit trap, a loop of willow designed to tighten when a rabbit stepped into it.

While Ragnald liked hunting, he wasn't about to kill a helpless animal with no chance of escape. A real warrior wouldn't do that, so using his sword he cut the fox free. It sprang away from him, obviously with no leg broken, then stood staring at him. "Off you go then," said Ragnald, sheathing his sword. He then made his way across the marsh but each time he looked back the fox was there looking back. Eventually it vanished.

One day, some months later, he was on the beach trying to remember the runes his mother was teaching him. He used his sword to mark them out on the sand and became so engrossed in his work that he failed to notice an approaching sea mist.

Suddenly he shivered. Cold! He looked up and fear struck his heart as he saw he was surrounded by a grey wall lit by a pearly light which was already starting to fade. Where were his stakes? He'd never find them in this and he daren't try and find his way across the marsh without them. He shouted even though he knew it was futile. No one would hear him out here and he'd not told anybody about his stakes. He shivered even harder as fear gripped him; a night out here was not to be contemplated. Time passed as it grew darker.

Then he saw it. A fox! Staring at him! He walked towards it as it moved into the mist then stopped and looked round at him. *It wants me to follow it,* thought Ragnald and did so, treading very cautiously. He came to the first of his stakes, then another. The fox was leading him out of the marsh!

Eventually, when Ragnald could dimly see the fires from the village where people were cooking their evening meal the fox, with one last look at him, darted away into the mist. He ran indoors.

"Oh there you are," said his mother, "we were getting worried." Ragnald blurted out the story of how the fox had saved him.

"Right," ordered his father, "now go and put your sword away; it's time to eat."

When he'd gone his mother said: "What an imagination! As if an animal would ever help a human!"

A Bare Problem

"She's out there again," said Brian to his wife, Rita, as he reached the bottom of the stairs.

"Well we can't do anything about it," she replied, "so we'll just have to put up with it until the weather changes or winter comes."

"Yes, but it's not right," he replied.

'She' was Mrs Jenkins next door who had taken it upon herself to sunbathe nude in her back garden.

It was not that Brian and Rita were prudes; it was just that their thirteen-and-a-half-year old son, Paul, found the attractions of Mrs Jenkins far more worthy of study than his homework which would often lie neglected while he gazed down and to the right from his bedroom window. Mrs Jenkins gave no sign of being aware of her admirer, unless she didn't care. She just lay on a blanket on the lawn, dozing to the strains of Radio 2 from the little radio at her side.

An appeal to Mr Jenkins produced no positive result. "My wife is on our private property," he had said. "You should stop your son from looking." Easier said than done although Brian did stop Paul taking his friends up for a gawk too.

This day was a Wednesday and Brian didn't work Wednesday afternoons or weekends. His business as a shoe maker/repairer wasn't so much in demand these days which is why he carried a stock of medium-priced trainers. He just about managed to keep the shop open four and a half days a week. Paul was at school, of course.

Brian and Rita settled down to a nice roast chicken dinner. As Brian's hobby was bird watching he found it ironic to be eating one bird while loving all the others.

After dinner, Rita went off to spend the afternoon with her mother while Brian, with binoculars and flask, set off to his hide in the trees which grew in the waste ground behind the houses, which were a terrace with the Jenkins' abode on the end.

Nothing much happened for a while. The inevitable sparrows and the odd pigeon. Then he noticed something odd. A bird which alternately hovered then moved from side to side. Brian looked through his binoculars. It was a drone, not a bird, and was hovering over the Jenkins' garden. Someone was spying on Mrs Jenkins!

An idea formed in Brian's head. He gathered up his binoculars and flask and hurried home. Once there he quickly went up to Paul's room.

Paul was one of a very rare species, a tidy teenager who kept all his old toys in pristine condition. Brian searched until he found the catapult, aluminium with 'Milbro' stamped on it. The elastic and leather pouch was still in good condition. He searched further until he found the bag of marbles.

He went to the window and opened it. Yes, there she was seemingly asleep with the radio drowning out any noise from the drone. Brian had to get this right. He didn't want the drone falling on Mrs Jenkins and hurting her.

At last, opportunity presented itself. He fired and missed. There were many more misses, the marbles ending up on the waste ground. Brian persevered and eventually got one good hit. One good hit was all that was needed to cause the drone to tilt and before its controller could react flew a diagonal path into the Jenkins' lawn, bounced off and crashed into the fence.

This woke Mrs Jenkins up and, seeing the drone, shouted to her husband. He came out and examined it, one propeller still whirring until its battery ran out. "This is a film camera," observed Mr Jenkins, "someone was filming you. Luckily it crashed else that would have been all over the internet tonight."

"I wonder who would do that?" said Mrs Jenkins.

"Probably that nuisance from next door," replied her husband.

Brian, who had been watching from the window, leaned out and shouted, "It wasn't me, it was me who shot it down with this," at the same time waving the catapult.

"Oh – er – thanks," said Mr Jenkins and turned his attention back to the drone.

After a time, he found the SD card, removed it and smashed it with a hammer and that was the end of Mrs Jenkins outdoor sunbathing. She bought an indoor sun bed instead.

The drone? Mr Jenkins handed it in to the police. It was never claimed.

Needs Must

Dan had it all worked out. A new, heavily advertised blockbuster film was coming to town and he, together with his wife Grace, were very much looking forwards to seeing it. "We'll need to get tickets in advance," he said, "We'll never get in otherwise." And so he did, for the matinee performance some three weeks hence.

Two weeks later his boss made an announcement to the whole office where he worked: "It's my 50th birthday next Saturday," he said, "and I've booked the Metropole for a party. You are all invited together with your spouses or partners and I shall expect to see you all there at eight 'o clock sharp."

Dan realised with gloom that this was the same day as the film. Grace would be very disappointed and he daren't miss the party as he was hoping for promotion. He phoned the theatre. Could he change the tickets to a different day? Sorry no, fully booked.

At home, he told Grace who voiced her dismay. "Everybody else is going," she wailed, "and they'll all be talking about it."

Then Dan realised something. "Wait a minute," he said excitedly, "the film finishes at seven and we don't have to be there until eight. It's only a twenty-minute taxi ride from the theatre to the hotel. We can easily do both." So great relief all round.

The great day arrived and Dan and Grace got a taxi to the theatre asking the driver to be back promptly at seven. Dan felt a bit conspicuous in his best suit and Grace in a new dress but that couldn't be helped.

The film over and the taxi waiting they set off. "Great film," said Dan, "and it all worked out fine." He spoke too soon.

The taxi suddenly stopped and traffic piled up behind. Just a sea of cars in front. After a few minutes, the driver called his base: "I'm stuck in the High Street with a fare," he said. "Any idea what the problem is?"

“Yes,” came the reply. “Jimmy’s just called in. Lorry overturned right across the road. You’ll be there for some time.”

Dan and Grace overheard all this and looked at each other glumly. “We can walk it,” said Grace, “but we’ll be late.”

“We can’t be,” responded Dan, “he’ll be furious.” He looked around, more in desperation than hope. Then he noticed something.

A nearby second-hand shop was just closing up, a man taking the goods displayed outside into the shop. One of them was a tandem.

“Pay the taxi,” said Dan, “then come on.”

He jumped out and ran to the shop. “How much for the tandem?” he asked. “’Undred and fifty quid, mate,” said the surprised man. Dan took out his wallet as Grace came hurrying up.

“What are you doing?” she asked.

“Buying this, it’s our only hope,” came the reply.

“You gonna ride it now?” said the man, looking at Dan’s suit and Grace’s dress. “It might need a bit of oil.”

“Forget that,” said Dan as he gave him the money, “we don’t want oil on our clothes.”

“I’ve never ridden a tandem,” cried Grace, a stricken look on her face.

“Then just keep your feet up off the pedals and let me pedal it,” ordered Dan.

The two mounted and set off on their wobbly, squeaky way leaving the man scratching his head at the easiest sale he’d ever made.

Dan and Grace made their way between the line of traffic easily enough and also through the traffic on the other side of the lorry. They’d had to dismount to get around that. They ignored the comments of pedestrians and other road users and got to the hotel with ten minutes to spare, leaving the tandem round the back. A quick smarten up in the loos and they were ready for the fray. The party was a great success and in the fullness of time Dan got his promotion.

The tandem? Oh, somebody nicked that!

A Helping Hand

Ferdinand N'Shombe was a happy man. Well, what man wouldn't be running a bar on the beach of a tropical island accompanied by a good wife?

It was only a small island, no airstrip or anything like that but it did have a decent harbour where the rich parked their yachts and a ferry from the mainland docked every week. This was how Ferdinand got his supplies, that and an ancient Land Rover that made the weekly 10 mile journey from the harbour across the island to the bar, its driver, Charles, looking forward to an ice-cold beer at the end of it. Most people had French names as the island was once a French possession.

Ferdinand had one regular customer who wasn't a native. Known only as Tyler he had a sort of half-Australian accent, called everybody 'mate' and also drank ice-cold beer.

One thing that did annoy Ferdinand was the youths of both sexes who hung around their small boats begging from the tourists when they weren't out in their boats fishing. Tyler would often give them a few dollars whereupon Ferdinand would frown and say: "You shouldn't encourage them, they're bad for trade."

"Aw, give 'em a break mate," would come the reply, "tourists expect it and it's only 'cos they ain't got no work."

"You mean they don't want any," Ferdinand would growl back.

One day a small girl came running up to the bar. Ferdinand recognised her as Nadine, one of Charles' daughters. Somewhat out of breath she panted: "Dada not come no more. The Rover him broke, caught on fire, no good now. Dada ok but he gonna put feet up, no work no more." And with that she departed.

"Oh no!" wailed Ferdinand to Tyler. "There isn't anyone else, what am I going to do?" He went into the back of the bar to impart the bad news to Juliette, his wife, so didn't see Tyler slip down to the gathering of youths.

When he emerged with a worried-looking Juliette, Tyler was back on his stool and the youths all stood near.

"What you want?" said Ferdinand crossly.

"We get bottles and stuff," said one of the boys.

Ferdinand stared. "How?" he said.

"We get bottles and stuff," replied the boy, "go round coast in boats, bring it here."

Ferdinand looked at Tyler. "Can I trust them?" he asked but before Tyler had a chance to answer the boy said indignantly: "We no steal, we get bottles and stuff good."

"Give 'em a go mate," said Tyler, "they'll come up good."

"Ok," said Ferdinand, "and I'll pay you what I paid Charles."

It worked fine. Juliette checked everything when the youths brought it in. Nothing was cracked, broken or missing. Ferdinand was impressed.

When the youths lined up for their money he said: "You do this every week? I pay you same." The youths jumped at it and it was the same from then on.

Tyler, after a long draught of cold beer commented: "Y'know mate, I've banged about this sad old world a bit and I've found it's generally true that if people are given a worth-while job with decent pay they'll come up to the mark all right."

"You'm be sure right," said Ferdinand, pouring himself a rum and coke.

A New Start

Fred Smith looked across the street yet again at the padlocked doors of his smithy and again smiled at the irony of having a name the same as his job. Except he didn't have a job anymore which had been the case for seven months now. Nobody wanted blacksmiths anymore and the few horses in the area were looked after by the farrier.

It was the same with gates and fences. People got them from the garden centre, machine made and all the same. No individuality, no craftsmanship and no job for Fred or his son who was about to leave school, intending to follow in his father's footsteps. Fred sighed, another day of trying to find something to do.

In the village hall, the committee were discussing the annual village fete in which they tried to do something different each year. Farmer White suggested a hog roast and offered to donate two suckling pigs ready gutted and cleaned. Everyone thought this an excellent idea and Mrs Jones volunteered her gas barbecue where they could roast sausages and also a medley of vegetables to accompany them and for those who didn't eat meat. Other matters being settled the committee adjourned to the local pub.

Time passed until just a week before the fete Jack Billings said: "The spits! We've forgotten the spits to roast the pigs on! We can't use wood; it would burn away before the pigs were cooked!" Panic! Then someone said: "Fred Smith!"

Fred perked up no end when he was told. "But metal," he said, "I've only got a few horseshoes." A pause, then Mr White said: "The cage!"

The cage was where the police used to keep dangerous dogs until the courts decided what should be done with them. It was at the back of the police station which had been closed and locked these past two years and was scheduled for demolition. "I know they intend to dump it," said Mrs Phillips whose son was a policeman.

Fred soon got his smithy open and he grabbed a hacksaw, a chisel and a hammer. He soon had a good selection of bars and sang to himself as he donned his old leather apron, boots, kerchief, and cap and fired up his forge.

Selecting four of the bars he heated one end of each one and beat it flat. After they cooled, he made a vertical cut in each then heated them again so he could bend each one into a graceful curl thus making an ornate V in each to support the spits. He then sharpened the other ends on his old treadle grindstone into points. Then more heat which enabled him to twist the bars into barley sugar shapes. For the two spits, he sharpened one end of each into a point. The other ends he re-heated and formed into S shapes, finishing with a wooden handle to protect the hand from the heat. At last, the two spits were finished and Fred stood back, well pleased with his efforts.

The fete was, as usual, a great success as was the hog roast. Volunteers took turns to rotate the spits, basting the pigs from time to time with Bovril diluted in water which produced a delicious black crackling.

One man, a stranger, stood looking at the spits for a while. He then approached a volunteer asking: "Excuse me, but who made these spits?"

"Fred Smith," the volunteer replied as he turned the handle.

"And where would I find him?" The stranger further enquired.

"Try the beer tent," came the answer. "You can't miss 'im. Big bloke, wears a red kerchief."

The stranger soon found Fred and introduced himself as Steve Hughes, proprietor of Hughes' Fine Oak Furniture. "I've just bought The Grange," he informed Fred, "and I want to change the gates and the fencing to a design individual to me. Being a craftsman myself I appreciate your skill. Would you like the job?"

Fred's eyes opened wide. He knew the Grange. A large house fenced around with low walls and pillars at intervals with wrought iron fencing between. Also at least two sets of gates. It would be a big job.

"Yes, I would love to do it," said Fred. "I'd need help but my son would do that."

"Right then," said Mr Hughes. "I can see this will take some time so I'll pay you a weekly retainer while work is in progress." He went on: "Come up to the house tomorrow and I'll show you some designs I've had done. 10 'o clock, okay?"

"I'll be there," Fred replied, "and thank you Mr Hughes." The two men shook hands and Mr Hughes left. Fred then phoned his old supplier, telling him he was back in business.

Work started and the village soon rang with the sound of hammers wielded by Fred and Jim, his son. The villagers were glad to see the old forge open again which was originally opened by Fred's great-grandfather.

Mr Hughes' recommendations to his many business contacts and friends brought Fred many more orders and a newly-painted sign 'Smith & Son' soon appeared above the Smithy.

Well, you can't keep a good man down for long, can you?

A Fright

Sheila and Rachel were two 27-year-old women who lived together, worked together and played together, an arrangement which suited them both very well. Their jobs were well paid so they were able to indulge themselves pretty well – within reason.

One day, while on holiday abroad, they hired a two-person jet ski and enjoyed it so much that they decided to buy one. A new jet ski was duly purchased plus a small trailer and a tow bar was fitted to their car. But then came a problem – the sea.

The sea, being unpredictable as to its wont, was often too rough for most things, especially jet skiing, so Sheila suggested they find a nice inland lake. A map soon produced several from which they chose a long, thin one.

To avoid other holidaymakers they decided to go a week before the schools broke up for the summer holidays and the holiday season proper started. The day of departure arrived and they set off with wet suits, bathing caps and spare fuel for the jet ski. Rachel even packed sun tan lotion 'just in case'.

At their destination, they checked into their hotel then walked the short distance to a small, cosy pub for dinner over which they planned the next day. "We'll go at the crack of dawn," said Sheila, "no one about then." The other regular customers, except one, took no notice; they were well used to strangers.

The exception was Hamish who did keep an ear cocked to the two women while talking to his companions. At closing time, the pub emptied and Hamish walked home. He went to his shed and checked his apparatus which hadn't been used for a couple of years. Well, it wouldn't do to overdo it. Satisfied, he went indoors and to his wife, Morag, said: "Reckon we'll have to open early this year," referring to the cafe cum souvenir shop they owned and ran.

The next morning dawned bright and calm and the jet ski was soon zooming up the lake with the two women on board. Reaching the end they turned to go back and at approximately the half-way stage screamed as one when ahead and to the left of them a huge head rose out of the water. It was what one might call dragonesque with glaring eyes, flaring nostrils and a gaping mouth full of gleaming white fangs. Behind it was part of a dark green body with a short line of triangular plates along it.

Sheila, who was steering, swerved to the right, giving the monster a wide berth. Rachel watched the fearsome head as it turned to watch their progress. Both women continued to scream until their jet ski beached and they were safely ashore.

Satisfied, Hamish, for it was he, swam behind some rushes, climbed out of the water and divested himself of his costume. He packed it into a little barrow and wheeled it back to his shed.

The women's screams brought a few other people out who listened with open mouths to the women's breathless explanations. The word quickly spread. "There's been another sighting!" The local, then national, newspapers reported it which soon brought a stream of cars and motorhomes to the area which disgorged people carrying cameras, camcorders, telescopes and binoculars.

The little cafe did a roaring trade keeping Hamish, Morag and their two daughters very busy. The elder, Fiona, said: "Ye'll get caught one day, Dad."

"Och no," replied Hamish. "Folks are fools and believe what they want to. Fools and their money are soon parted."

As for the jet ski it was sold together with its trailer and the tow bar was removed. Sheila and Rachel found other diversions the following year, their friends remaining in awe of them and their sighting of the Loch Ness Monster.

Best Friends

Myself and Roy had been best friends from school. You could say we grew up together and we shared a common interest in most things, one of them being astronomy.

The problem with astronomy is that, ideally, you need a cold, crisp, clear night for the best sky watching with no heat haze to make things shimmer and as neither of us are winter people we confined our interest to books, television programmes and the internet, sometimes preferring the cosiness of our local.

One day an excited Roy met me at home with the news that a really good meteor shower was due in two weeks' time. These showers, known as radiants, occur at regular times of the year and vary in their intensity. A good one can produce a spectacular display.

"But it's the middle of October," I said, "It'll be freezing."

"We'll take my tent," said Roy. "You know I've got all the gear from our summer holidays." By 'our' he meant his family, camping had never appealed to me. Roy's enthusiasm was infectious so I agreed; secretly hoping it would be cloudy that week. I made one stipulation; no alcohol as I would drive there and Roy would drive back, to which he agreed.

Well, the clouds let me down by staying away so we loaded up my 4x4 with Roy's huge eight berth tent, sleeping bags and all the other gear and set off. Our wives thought we were mad.

Roy seemed to have developed a cough and occasionally took a little swig from a large bottle of cough mixture he produced from his rucksack.

"Are you sure you're OK?" I asked.

"Yes," he replied, "just keep away; I don't want you to catch it."

We duly drove way out of town and pitched camp on top of a hill. A very cold night with no wind.

Over the next two nights we saw plenty of meteors but it was cold and I found myself looking forward to the end of the week.

I got very suspicious about Roy's cough. It never seemed to get any better or worse and I noted how carefully he stowed his bottle away after using it. I determined to investigate.

The next morning I waited until Roy had popped out to the bushes as it were and examined the bottle. It was whisky! He'd cheated! I felt very angry and determined to confront him but then I had a better idea.

When he came back, I said I was just going to pop to the village for cigarettes. I did so but I also bought a bottle of cough mixture from the little chemists.

Back at camp I again waited until Roy was out of the way then grabbed his bottle, noted it was half-full, then emptied it well away from the tent, re-filling it half-full with cough mixture.

He came back and in due course his 'cough' did too. He retrieved his bottle and took a good swig upon which he developed a real cough and watering eyes. "You swine!" he at last spluttered. "How dare you sneak in my rucksack!"

"You shouldn't cheat!" I shouted back. "I said no alcohol – you were supposed to drive home!"

The rest of the day was spent in a glowering silence. Night fell and we lay on our sleeping bags with no inclination to move, meteors or not. In the light of our battery lamp, I could see him looking at me. Finally he said:

"Are you cold?"

"Yes," I replied.

"The pubs are still open," he said.

I looked at him and we both burst out laughing together. The tent and gear were quickly bundled into my 4x4 and we were soon warm and happy in the convivial atmosphere of our local.

We walked home. I picked the car up the next day. Our wives called us softies for the next few days. We still retained our astronomical interest – interest of the armchair kind.

Well, you can't beat a good friendship!

A Reunion

Robin hummed to himself as he drove his Jaguar; he was looking forward to the next two weeks.

He was born and grew up in a village near Manchester but had moved away from there many years ago.

Whilst there as a lad a group of them had found an old derelict house in the woods which soon became the base for their operations. They played soldiers and hide-an-seek or had picnics and just generally lazed about around a camp fire. Those going to hide always went in pairs; the house was too creepy to go on one's own.

As they grew girls joined them, usually the sisters of one or the other. Then they would just hang around, smoking cigarettes when they were too young to smoke and drinking lager from cans, also illegally.

Time passed and they all gradually went their separate ways leaving the house to its own devices. Robin married but tragically lost his wife early to cancer, leaving him, with the help of two sets of parents, to bring up their daughter alone.

Robin had always enjoyed writing and over time wrote a detective novel. More on a whim than any real hope of publication he sent it to a publisher who, to Robin's delight, enthused over it. The book was a great success encouraging him to write more, all of which brought him great financial reward.

One day he thought a move from the industrial midlands would be a good idea so he and his daughter, Gina, moved to Weymouth on the south coast. Gina soon made friends with whom she spent a lot of time on the beach or in the disco which is where she met a very special friend, a Scots lad named Duncan McRae. They kept in touch after he'd gone home and after Gina had been to visit him they became very close and married a year later.

They bought a small house at Stonehouse, which is just east of the M74 about 12 miles below Glasgow. Robin was sorry to see her go but wished them luck. “Never mind, Dad,” said Gina, “let us get settled then you can come and visit.”

And so Robin was driving there as he didn’t like public transport and was very much looking forward to spending the next two weeks with Gina and Duncan. A very long journey so he’d decided to break it for one night in Manchester then the next day he’d go and look at the old house – if it was still there. He hadn’t seen it for over 30 years.

The next morning, after a decent bed and breakfast, he found the right lane into the woods, parked up, and walked to its end. The house was still there but even more derelict than before. The window frames were missing and brambles almost covered one side. As he looked the memories came flooding back. Then to his surprise a woman appeared.

Despite being in his own age group, he recognised her immediately. “Jessica Simmonds,” he said. “Good lord, fancy meeting you hero.”

“Hello Robin,” she replied “and it’s Jessica Green now. I still live in the village but my husband runs the shop now. Green’s the Greengrocer, that’s funny, isn’t it?”

Robin thought that was a bit of an odd thing to say and as they talked he thought there was something odd about her although he couldn’t put his finger on it. They talked and reminisced for some time, remembering times and people from long past but at last Robin had to go as he was now late. Back on the road he determined to look up Jessica again.

After a very enjoyable two weeks, he was back again but in the village this time. After a look at the house, he grew up in he found the shop and went in. A man of his own age was behind the counter. “Could I speak to Mrs Green?” he asked.

The man stared at him, frowning. “What?” he asked in return.

“Mrs Jessica Green,” said Robin, “I knew her as a child, we both grew up here.”

“I’m sorry,” said Mr Green, relaxing, “but my wife’s been dead this last four years.” Robin’s mouth dropped open.

“But I was talking to her two weeks ago,” he said. “Up at that old house we used to play in.”

The frown returned. "I know about the house," Mr Green said. "Jessica told me about it but you must be mistaken." A customer came in and he turned away from Robin who then left the shop utterly bewildered.

Back in his car he thought about Jessica. He had seen her, he knew he had. But then he suddenly remembered what was odd about her.

She'd had no shadow.

Everything Comes to He Who Waits

Tommy was an avid book reader and had been for as long as he could remember starting with picture books, then comics, short stories and at last full-length books, a few fiction, but mainly non-fiction. By the time he was in his early twenties, he'd read books on almost every subject under the sun from astronomy to the Zulu wars and each morning as he cycled to work he tried to remember as much as he could from his readings of the previous evening. He could think about them at work too.

Tommy worked in the despatch department of a large mail order company and his job was to sort the outgoing parcels into their different areas so they went on to the correct delivery vans. Not a difficult task so plenty of time to think.

Tommy lived with his parents in an end house of a terrace. Joined at one side but a large gap on the other until the next house. One day he got curious about the gap and asked his father why it was there. His father said:

"These houses were built in 1903 by two builders who both started at the far ends. When they got to the middle, they found that one or both of them had miscalculated and the gap wasn't wide enough for two houses. They blamed each other for the error and argued over who was to build the one house. The argument was never settled even after at least one court case. The builders eventually moved on and the whole thing was forgotten. They both died long ago and so it has remained ever since."

The next day Tommy thought about what his father had said. Something he'd read years before was nagging at him. That evening he went from work to his local library where he consulted a certain book.

The next weekend found Tommy in the gap with his dad's strimmer, rubber gloves, a trowel and a plastic bag setting to work to tidy up the overgrown dog's toilet the gap had become. Brambles needed more than a strimmer so he used secateurs to cut them into manageable lengths then a fork to dig out the roots.

At last, the gap looked presentable, taking more than one weekend to make it so and more than a few evenings. The neighbours were impressed although they felt Tommy was mad to expend so much energy on it. They thought him even madder when he built a small shed on it in which he stored many of his books and even slept in it sometimes, returning to his house in the morning for a shave and breakfast.

His parents didn't interfere. Tommy seemed normal enough and at least it got his nose out of books as he continually tidied the ground in the gap.

The years rolled by and Tommy came to be regarded as something of a local eccentric. At the end this period, he was seen to go off one day dressed in his best suit carrying proof of identity and photographs of the gap of the before and after variety. His parents were mystified but said nothing.

Then one day a bulky letter arrived for Tommy marked 'Land Registry'. Upon opening it, he whooped with joy. "I've got it!" he cried.

"Got what?" asked his mother.

"The land in the gap!" he replied excitedly. "Squatter's rights! The land in the gap is now mine!" He showed his parents the deeds and other documents, all in his name.

"Well I'm blowed," said his father, "so that's what you were up to."

"Yes," said Tommy, "and now I'm going to sell it and we can use the money for a deposit on a house of our own so we won't have to pay rent anymore."

And there you have a good example of enterprise and patience paying off and Tommy back to his books of course!

A Fine Romance

Gerald and Amy had been together for the best part of eight years. They got on fine and were very comfortable and in love with each other, spending many an evening with a bottle of wine and listening to their extensive music collection.

The only fly in the ointment, as they say, was marriage. If Amy raised the subject, as she did from time to time, Gerald would say: "Plenty of time yet."

"No, there isn't," she would retort, "I'm 28 and I'd hoped to have kids by now."

"I'll think about it," he would say but that would be it, until the next time Amy raised it.

Gerald's hobby was keeping fit while Amy's was hang gliding and when the weather was right they'd combine the two. After driving to the top of a local inland cliff Gerald would help Amy set her glider up then watch her take flight. Then he'd run back down the road and along the base of the cliff then climb up it to where they'd started and wait for Amy who would often be on her second flight by then. He had done this many times before so knew the climb well. But not today.

About two thirds of the way up he stopped to wave at Amy as she glided some way above and she waved back. He then reached up to the next piece of protruding rock and to his horror it broke off and landed with a crack on the stones below. He was stuck! He now could not climb further and was not prepared to attempt to descend as he couldn't see his footholds. No one heard his shouts so he just had to wait until someone noticed him. That someone was Amy.

After soaring around for a further ten minutes or so, she deemed it time to land. Heading towards the cliff she saw Gerald still in the same place she'd seen him before. *He must be stuck,* she thought as panic rose within her.

She quickly landed, took off her helmet and harness and ran to the cliff edge. A thought struck her as she did so. At the edge, she lay on her stomach and peeped over. Gerald was about 30 feet down and obviously stuck.

Regaining her feet she ran to their car and called for help on her mobile then back to the cliff edge, lying prone once more. “Gerry!” she shouted, “are you stuck?”

He looked up and shouted: “Yes! Get help!”

She shouted back: “Will you marry me?”

“What? Get help!”

“Will you marry me?” she shouted again.

A pause, then: “Yes! Now get help!”

It may not have been the world’s strangest marriage proposal but it surely must have been close. And it had worked!

Help arrived and a girl abseiled down with a belt and rope for Gerald who was soon hauled up. After downing half a bottle of mineral water he thanked everyone profusely, saying: “I’ve never been so scared in my life. That’s it, my climbing days are over, I’ll stick to the gym in future.”

The drive home, with Amy’s glider stowed on the roof of the car, was mainly in silence except for Amy saying: “I’m giving up gliding.” To which she got no reply. At home, the silence was maintained until Gerald said: “If I’d said ‘no’, would you still have called for help?”

“I’d already done so,” she replied, “before I shouted down to you.”

His eyes widened. “You crafty so and so.”

“I suppose it was a bit mean taking advantage like that,” she said. “Look, you don’t have to if you don’t want to.”

“No,” came the reply and to her delight he said: “I said I would so I will.”

And so it was. A bridal gown, church, guests, reception, cake, disco – all the works. Children? Well, the wedding was only last Saturday so we’ll just have to wait and see!

Someone's Lucky Day

Paul was driving rather faster than he usually did, not a good idea as the country lanes which led from his house were rather narrow and winding in places. But he was late.

He was on his way to repair a roof for a customer who lived some 12 miles away but heavy rain was forecast for this afternoon so he needed to get the job done this morning. His wife, Wendy, had got him up in plenty of time and after breakfast he'd loaded his van with tiles, cement and sand plus ladders on the roof. Five miles away from home he realised he'd forgotten his tools, which he never left in his van overnight.

Now, after going back for them and trying to make up time, he approached a sharp left-hand bend he knew well. His tyres squealed as he started to take it but as he went round he was suddenly confronted by two magpies pecking away at roadkill. Instinctively he straightened up and braked but still ended up in the hedge on the far side of the road. The two startled birds flew away. Paul backed up onto the thankfully quiet road and inspected his van. A dented offside wing and a few scratches. He'd got away light.

At the job, he got to work straight away, thinking about the two magpies as he did so. That old rhyme came into his head:

One for sorrow,
Two for joy.
Three for a girl, Four for a boy. Five for silver, Six for gold.
Seven for a secret.
Never to be told.
Magpie!

Two for joy, he thought. *Maybe it's an omen!* That day, being Wednesday, was bingo night and also the night of the big prize.

The bingo club that he and Wendy went to was part of a country-wide chain of similar establishments. Once each month they were all linked together from a central location, the numbers being displayed on a large screen in each hall. The first person to get a full house won £10,000.

Paul imagined he'd won it. Two for joy, he'd saved two, perhaps they'd reward him in some way! Two weeks in Blackpool with Wendy would be nice, the illuminations, the tower, fish and chips, ice cream, lager yes, very nice. He got the job done just as the first raindrops began to fall. His trip home was taken with care as it lashed down.

That evening found Paul and Wendy together with about 50 others seated in the bingo hall, heads bent over their cards as the main event came up. The caller shouted out each number as it appeared on the screen. Paul's card slowly filled as the excitement within him mounted. What a surprise for Wendy!

Eventually only one number was left on his card, the number 2 – another omen! His tension was very high. But the next number called was not 2, it was 17 and to Paul's horror a female voice shouted: "House!"

Fifty heads jerked upright and a buzz of conversation broke out. The caller stepped down to check the lady's card leaving Paul praying it was an error. But it wasn't and the caller said: "It's a full house! Well done, madam, stand up and take a bow!" The lady, somewhat red-faced did so and everybody else applauded. Paul did too, despite feeling sick. He recognised the lady, she lived in the same street as Paul and Wendy.

Her Christian name?

Yes, you've guessed it.

It was Joy.

Luck Plays a Part

Roy Clarke was one of those people who never seemed to have any luck. He'd invested a pound or two in the National Lottery every week since it started but hadn't won even a tenner or a free go. Raffle prizes eluded him too and his Sunday evening bingo sessions at his local social club in the company of his wife were likewise barren, although his wife, Carol, did win once or twice.

At work during the lunch hour, he might put a pound's worth of 5ps in the fruit machine in his local cafe but get none of them back out while the next person to try would get the jackpot with their first coin!

His Saturday round of golf was often ruined by bad weather even though the previous week had been sunny and he wasn't one of those people who play out in all weathers.

At 55 years of age, without winning anything you might think Roy would have given up long ago but no, he remained optimistic that his luck would change. He wanted to be able to buy Carol a nice fitted kitchen and he'd always wanted a wood burning stove but the expense of lining the chimney was too much and Carol wouldn't countenance hire purchase or a bank loan.

One day it all changed.

Roy worked for a very large firm of builders who contracted for very large projects such as complete housing estates. He drove a machine which had caterpillar tracks which he called his 'crane'. While it could be used to pick things up, it was usually used to dig footings.

Roy liked his job. Snug in his cab in the cold or wet or with the side windows open in the heat he dumped the spoil in the back of a tipper lorry where another guy stood in the back and smoothed it out, a boring job which nobody liked especially in bad weather. And so it was when Roy's luck changed.

One morning Roy's mate didn't turn up. The foreman, a large, red-faced man called Huggins whom nobody liked, said: "Right, Clarke. I'll do the digging, you're in the lorry." So work started and of course it started to rain.

Just before lunch a cold and miserable Roy spotted something gleaming in the dirt. He pulled it out. It was about the size and shape of a large horseshoe, round in section with an ornate finial at each of the open ends. It was made of many intertwined strips of yellow metal! Which Roy noticed was untarnished. “Gold?” Thought a suddenly excited Roy. He put the object into his lunch bag, glad that Huggins, who was busy digging, hadn’t noticed. He carefully checked the spot and the load that followed but there was nothing else. He knew he should report the find.

Lunch time came and instead of the usual visit to the snug warmth of the cafe Roy drove his old car into town, parked, and went into the police station.

The desk sergeant’s eyes bulged when he saw and recognised the object. “This ’ere’s a gold torc,” he said. “Ancient people’s chiefs wore them round their necks. You need to report that to the coroner, ’is office is next door.”

In the coroner’s office, full details were taken of Roy, how and where he’d found the torc which was taken into the coroner’s care and for which Roy was given a receipt. All this made Roy late back to work to the annoyance of Huggins who yelled: “Where the ’ell ’ave you bin?”

At Roy’s explanation, Huggins’ mouth dropped open as he realised he would have been the one to find the torc had he left Roy to work the ‘crane’ and had done the smoothing himself.

In due course, the torc was declared Treasure Trove of course. The firm for who Roy worked owned the land from which the torc had come and they waived their share of the reward in Roy’s favour who ‘copped the lot’ as they say. So the new kitchen and log burner were duly fitted and Roy loved his new chore of splitting logs.

So, Nil desperandum! You never know what lies around the corner!

The Magic Puzzle

Billy liked jigsaw puzzles. He liked other things too, his favourite red jumper, his mum's cooking, his dad who took him to see football on Saturdays, even his teacher at school. But there was nothing he liked better than to be in his room with a glass of milk, a couple of chocolate hobnobs and a nice jigsaw puzzle.

One day in the summer Billy was walking with his parents in a strange town. They'd been there for a week on holiday and this was their last day, having a last look round before heading home.

Then Billy spotted a charity shop. He knew charity shops were often a good source of jigsaw puzzles. He stopped to look in the window as his parents walked on. Yes! A pile of jigsaws at the back of the shop with a card which read: '50p each'.

Billy checked the last of his holiday money. Yes, he had enough left for a puzzle and an ice-cream so he ran after his parents to ask if he could buy a puzzle.

"Yes," said his mother, "we'll wait for you and make sure it's all there."

Billy ran back to the shop, went in and looked through the pile until he found one he liked very much. The picture on the box showed a little girl about Billy's age and a little dog. She had one arm upraised with a ball in her hand while the little dog was up on its hind legs with shining eyes and tongue hanging out obviously waiting for her to throw it. They were in scenery of lovely green fields. To the left was a stream with a little bridge over it and to the right a copse of trees.

Billy sighed. He had often wished he's had a brother or sister and there were no nice fields where he lived.

The word 'complete' was written on the back of the box so Billy paid the lady shopkeeper 50p and she put the puzzle in a bag. Billy ran out to join his parents.

At home, it was supper and straight to bed after such a long journey.

The next day, which was a Sunday, Billy worked all day on his puzzle and at last, after tea, he finished it. He looked at the picture it made, which was obviously the same as the one on the box lid, and felt a bit sad. "I wish I could play with you," he said out loud, then Whoosh! And he found himself standing in front of the little girl!

She lowered her arm and the little dog dropped onto all four paws and looked from one to the other, his little stump of a tail wagging furiously.

"Hallo," said the little girl. "My name's Dora and this is my dog Jack. What's your name?"

For a moment, Billy was speechless, then he stammered: "B-B-Billy. What am I doing here?"

"Because you asked to come here," she replied. "You've done the magic puzzle, haven't you?"

"I didn't know it was magic," said Billy.

"Well, there you are," said Dora. "Would you like to play with us?"

"Oh, yes," said Billy excitedly and off they went having fun together. They threw the ball for Jack time after time although he never seemed to get tired of fetching it. They chased each other over the little bridge and back again then played hide-and-seek in the woods.

Billy, showing off as boys do, climbed a tree but when he came down he saw his red jumper had a green stain on it from the tree bark. "Oh no!" he said, "My mum will be cross."

"That's okay," said Dora, "the green belongs here so it won't go with you when you go back."

Then Billy suddenly realised his absence from home. "Mum!" he exclaimed in a worried voice, "She'll wonder where I've got to. How do I get back?"

"Just say you want to go home," replied Dora, "but she won't know you've been away because there's no time in a puzzle."

"What do you mean?" queried Billy.

"Have you even done a puzzle more than once?" asked Dora.

"Course I have," said Billy, "lots of times."

"Well, the picture's always the same, isn't it?" said Dora, "because there's no time in a puzzle."

"Oh," said Billy, not worried any more. "But I'd better go. Can I come and play again?" he asked hopefully.

"Yes," said Dora, "as often as you like."

"Will I always be able to come?" said Billy.

"No," replied Dora. "When you go back to your own time, time will start again and one day you'll grow too big to play with me. But we can have lots of fun before that."

"Oh, right," said Billy, pleased. "I'll see you tomorrow then." Then: "I want to go home," and Whoosh! He was back in his room in front of his puzzle again.

But wait! There was something else! A little boy in the puzzle wearing a red jumper! He had his back turned so you couldn't see his face.

Just then Billy's mother came in. "Bedtime." She said as she looked at the puzzle. "That's a nice picture," she said, "and that little boy looks just like you!"

Billy didn't say anything, he just grinned to himself.

It was his secret. And he was keeping it!

A Problem Solved

Alan and Susan were together with their parents on holiday. At 13 Susan was the elder while at 11 Alan was very much the younger brother. Not that Susan was bossy in the way many big sisters are but she did tend to take charge when they went out together which wasn't too often. At home they both got on well enough and were quite fond of each other but they both had their own friends and hobbies. Alan's was football; he was goalkeeper for his local boy's team.

Their holiday venue was the seaside with good sea views from the hills that surrounded their holiday chalet. They both looked forward to the days that were to follow, what a nice change from the overcrowded town where they lived!

As they were old enough to look after each other their parents were quite happy to leave them to their own devices with the usual admonitions to be careful after giving them some spending money. So off they went to find any adventure that might present itself.

It was a hot day and they walked a long way finally coming to a road with a sign that said a lighthouse lay that way. "Let's try that," said Susan, "I like lighthouses."

The road led up a long hill and as they walked, taking in the sights and sounds of the sea, Alan thought about his problem. "I don't know what to write," he said.

"Oh you'll think of something," replied Susan.

This problem was the last part of a series of exams, the passing of which would get Alan into grammar school where he desperately wanted to go. He was confident he'd done pretty well in the other subjects but it was the essay that was causing him great concern. He knew the rules of football of course, but nothing about the history of the game.

They came to a cafe but the crowded car park caused them to walk on.

The top of the hill was reached at last and joy! An ice-cream van! An ice-cold Lilt followed by a 99 each went down very well indeed. Looking around they found the lighthouse way below them perched on a little island of rock which was reached across a little bridge. A small house adjoined the lighthouse; both were painted a glaring white.

"Let's go down, it'll be an adventure," said Susan excitedly but then she noticed a sign fixed to the wall which said: 'Visits to the lighthouse. Tickets available from the cafe.' So that seemed to be the end of that. But then a man appeared.

"Ullo you two young 'uns'," he said, "Goin' down?"

"No," said Alan and Susan in unison, "we didn't get tickets."

"Tell you what," said the man, "My name is James Jones and I'm the lighthouse keeper. I'll take you down free – just this once mind."

"Oh, thank you," said two young voices, again in unison. An adventure after all!

At the little house Mr. Jones' wife appeared, a smiling plump lady who hailed from Devon. "Allo my 'andsomes'," she said in a voice that was pleased to see them. "You're just in time for tea, little 'uns your age are always hungry."

Tea was freshly baked scones with great dollops of clotted cream and strawberry jam. Tea for the adults, cold lemonade for their guests. Normally the Jones charged for this, but not today.

While they ate Mr Jones started to tell them about the lighthouse and Alan, remembering his essay asked: "Could I borrow a pen and paper please?" Mr Jones produced them and Alan made notes as he talked. How they used lighthouses in the old days, that ours were attacked by German aircraft in World War II and that the current one was automatic with special lenses in the lamp called Fresnel lenses. Keeping them clean was one of Mr Jones' duties.

Then it was a tour of the lighthouse and more note-taking by Alan.

At last, it was time to go and after many grateful thanks two tired children made their happy way back to the chalet and their parents, eager to hear about their day.

Back at school Alan's essay on lighthouses and their history passed with flying colours. "Well done," said his teacher, "you must have done a lot of research."